Futures

A compilation of short stories from young
writers from around the world

Published and distributed by:

Voices of Future Generations Children's Initiative (VoFG CI)

www.vofg.org

Edited by Nico Cordonier Gehring

Layout: Steiner Graphics

Copyright © 2025 by VoFG CI

ISBN: 978-1-998850-39-6

Voices of Future Generations Children's Initiative

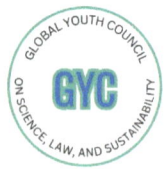

Futures

A compilation of short stories from young writers from around the world

Edited by Nico Cordonier Gehring

Voices of Future Generations Children's Initiative

A Voices of Future Generations Book

Acknowledgements

All my gratitude is due to Dr. Odette Lara-Morales, Elianys Martinez and Phoebe McElligott of the Voices of Future Generations Children's Initiative for all their guidance, encouragement and support, and to Baroness Julie Smith of Newnham, Mr Alistair Henfrey, Professor Freya Baetens, Professor Pamela Towela Sambo, Professor Marie-Claire Cordonier-Segger and Max Lee, for their careful review, insights and wisdom as judges. My deepest appreciation is also due to August Deeming for his collaboration. I would also like to thank and acknowledge the other leaders of the Global Youth Council on Science, Law and Sustainability for their engagement, enthusiasm and inspiration.

Nico Cordonier Gehring,
Editor of Futures
Cambridge, United Kingdom 2025

To the children who speak up so that the voices of our generation can be heard.

Preface

By Prof David Boyd

Children and youth are among the most vulnerable groups in society, yet they hold the greatest potential to shape the future of our world. The Sustainable Development Goals (SDGs), adopted by the United Nations in 2015, represent a bold and transformative agenda to create a sustainable, equitable, and just future for all. Central to achieving this vision is the recognition and protection of children's rights, as enshrined in the United Nations Convention on the Rights of the Child (CRC) and other human rights instruments. These rights are not merely aspirations—they are legal and moral obligations that demand urgent and sustained action by governments at all levels, businesses, and other duty bearers.

The SDGs and children's rights are deeply inter-connected. Each of the 17 goals—from eradicating poverty and hunger to ensuring quality education, clean water, and a safe climate—is rooted in human rights law and addresses critical aspects of well-being for children and youth. Yet, the challenges we face today are truly immense, ranging from the triple planetary crisis to chronic poverty and the rising tide of right-wing populism. Millions of young people are denied their fundamental human rights due to conflict, environmental degradation, and systemic inequalities. The climate crisis, in particular, poses an existential threat, disproportionately affecting the physical and mental health, well-being, and future prospects of children and youth who bear no responsibility for the crisis yet suffer its gravest consequences.

Set against this foreboding backdrop, *Futures* is both timely and essential. It illuminates the key connections between the SDGs and human rights. Many of the tales offer diverse and creative ideas about how to empower young people and fulfil our shared commitments. The book provides a dazzling diversity of inspiring stories that also confront the conditions that perpetuate inequality, injustice and unsustainable actions. Above all, it emphasizes the voices of children and youth themselves—voices that must be at the centre of our collective efforts to build a better world. When young people speak, older generations must listen, and act.

As we already have passed the halfway point of the 2030 Agenda, we must acknowledge that our progress is not sufficient. Not even close. Transformative changes are urgently needed, guided by the principles of equity, inclusion, and sustainability. The stories in this book serve as an eloquent and compelling call to action for policymakers, educators, advocates, and all who believe in the power of collective action to create a brighter future. By prioritizing the rights of young people and embedding these rights in every aspect of sustainable development, we not only fulfill our obligations but also invest in a world where all can thrive.

The right to a clean, healthy, and sustainable environment is a fundamental pillar of this vision. It is a right that belongs to everyone, everywhere, regardless of where they are born and without discrimination. The right to a healthy environment, embraced wholeheartedly by children and youth around the world, represents one of the most powerful tools available to protect Nature, the life support system for humans and millions of other species with whom we share this beautiful blue-green planet. As global citizens, we have a responsibility to ensure that no one is left behind—and that includes safeguarding future generations from the twin crises of environmental destruction and social inequality.

I hope that this book will inspire and empower you to take bold, innovative, and compassionate steps toward a world where the rights of children and youth are fully realized, and the SDGs are understood as not merely a political promise but a set of binding obligations firmly founded on international human rights law. We must do everything within our power to transform the SDGs from a glittering dream into lived reality for all.

Ultimately, *Futures* is a book about love—love for our families, our friends and our fellow humans, and love for the miraculous and unique Earth that we are so immensely fortunate to call home.

Foreword

By Prof. Pamela Towela Sambo

In a world increasingly interconnected and interdependent, the aspirations embodied in the Sustainable Development Goals (SDGs) provide a powerful blueprint for a just and equitable future. Among these, the rights of children and youth as enshrined in the UN Convention on the Rights of the Child and the UN system of human rights stand as the cornerstones, reminding us of our collective responsibility to ensure that the youngest members of our societies not only survive but thrive.

This collection of award-winning stories brings to life the vision, courage and imagination of youth whose voices are too often unheard, demonstrating the transformative power of their ideals and aspirations in the global agenda. Each story reveals the intersection of the SDGs with the rights of children—showing how education, health, gender equality, access to water and energy, climate action are not unrealistic dreams, but part of an indivisible commitment to human dignity.

Through these narratives, we witness the resilience, ingenuity, and determination of young leaders and the communities that champion their rights. These stories reflect the challenges faced by marginalized children and youth from rural villages to urban settlements, and highlight the opportunities that arise when governments, civil society, and individuals work together to fulfil the promise of the SDGs. Importantly, the stories remind us that young people are not mere recipients or beneficiaries, but active participants and agents of change. Their dreams, actions, and ideas serve as a call to action for all stakeholders to amplify their voices and ensure no one is left behind.

It is my hope that this collection will inspire readers to reimagine the possibilities of a world where the rights of children and youth are fully realised, and the SDGs are achieved. May these stories ignite a renewed sense of urgency to address the systemic inequities that deny children and youth their fundamental rights and galvanize collective action to create a future where everyone can grow, learn, and contribute in dignity. Together, we can turn these stories of struggle and resilience into a shared commitment to justice, sustainability, and hope for generations to come.

It has been such an honourable task working with terrific children on the Voices of Future Generations Children's Initiative (VoFG CI) and the Global Youth Council. Judging all the wonderful sustainability stories was so fulfilling yet so difficult because all perspectives accurately spoke to the importance of empowering future generations now

As Chairperson of the Human Rights Commission of Zambia, I am particularly pleased that children's inspirational stories are drawn from across Africa and other parts of the world, bearing testimony that children's rights are indeed starting with the children themselves.

Table of Contents

Contributor Biographies

Editor

Nico Cordonier Gehring is Vice-Chair of the Global Youth Council for Science, Law, and Sustainability, a young historian, geographer, and climate activist. He is editor of the blog, nicosnaturalworld.org, a founding co-chair of Cambridge Schools Eco-Council, and an active leader in the Sustainability Society of Winchester College, where he is a scholar. Nico is also a UN Child Ambassador for the Sustainable Development Goals with the UNESCO Voices of Future Generations Children's Initiative, and an award-winning young author whose stories are published in the Luna Spark anthologies, winning first place in the world for 2022. A laureate of the UK Young Environmentalist and the Cambridgeshire Inspirational Young Stars Environmental awards, Nico enjoys drama, music, kayaking and speaking up for nature.

Preface Author

Professor David Boyd is an associate professor of law, policy, and sustainability at the University of British Columbia and former UN Special Rapporteur on human rights and the environment. Ecological lawyer, policy advisor for governments and NGOs, author of nine books (e.g. The Environmental RIghts Revolution, The Optimistic Environmentalist, The Rights of Nature, Unnatural Law, Cleaner, Greener, Healthier) and 100+ articles, Professor David Boyd advocates for the right to a healthy and sustainable environment and the rights of nature.

Foreword Author

Professor Pamela Towela Sambo is an environmental lawyer and professor who specialises in the legal aspects of environmental justice, EIAs and human rights. With twenty-five years of experience in Zambian law practice and research, she is a passionate advocate for research and community empowerment, environmental awareness, human rights, and constitutional law. She is currently the Head of the Private Law Department at the University of Zambia and the Chairperson of the Human Rights Commission.

Authors

Nana Aisha Bello Abdulkadir is a sixteen-year-old young author from Nigeria, an avid reader, and a devoted Muslim. She has started self publishing on online platforms, including Wattpad and Medium. She aspires to be a published author and an English teacher. Her greatest achievement is knowing her stories bring a smile to people's faces.

Sanika Addri is a seventh grade student from Bangladesh who studies at the Netherhall School, Cambridge, in the United Kingdom. She is a member of the school book club and has been awarded a 'Certificate of Distinction' (Juniors 10-12) in the UK Bebras Challenge 2023 organised by Raspberry Pi Foundation in partnership with the University of Oxford and Bebras. She was also awarded a 'Bronze Certificate' in 2023 from the United Kingdom Mathematics Trust (UKMT). She has completed four years of courses in art, music and dance at the Bulbul Academy of Fine Arts (BAFA), Bangladesh. Her hobbies include reading, writing stories, and watching movies. She also likes to listen to music and create content for her YouTube channel.

Mary Adwo Ansah is a seventeen-year-old student of the renowned Krobo Girls' Presbyterian SHS. She is the second daughter of Mr. Paul Ansah and Ms. Vivian Mantebea. She has a keen interest in reading, writing, and drawing.

Carina Araujo is a twelve-year old Brazilian-American writer and artist, who studies at Barnesville School of Arts and Sciences in the United States. Two of the five books she wrote and illustrated won the WETA PBS Kids Writers Contest. She won haiku contests in 2022 and 2023 organized by the Martin Luther King Jr. Memorial Library in Washington D.C. and several awards for her drawings that raise awareness of environmental issues and were featured in public transportation, storm drains, and galleries and libraries.

Sarah Bahraki is an Afghan refugee in the United Kingdom and a first-year undergraduate at King's College London, specializing in International Development. She founded Action for SDG4 Community, focusing on educational advocacy and opportunities, particularly for Afghan girls. She serves as a Delegate for Democracy Without Borders and a Global Youth Ambassador for their World Organization, alongside board roles at Unite2030. Recently, she represented UN Woman UK at CSW68 and delivered a keynote at the UN Youth Forum, following remarks by UN Secretary-General Antoniou Gutrish.

Carlos Andres Olivera Caballero is an Indigenous activist from Santa Cruz de la Sierra, Bolivia. He volunteers at "La Cuchilla" Regional Library and founded Bookcubers. Fluent in Spanish, English, and Guaraní, Carlos Andres holds multiple technical diplomas and is an active member of Santa Cruz's Global Shapers Hub and Youth Council. He has received numerous awards for activism, leadership, and academic excellence.

Jona David is co-chair of the Global Youth Council on Science, Law, and Sustainability, as well as a senior editor of Harmony Online Journal, currently studying at Cambridge University. He has published four books and is an alum of the UNESCO Voices of Future Generations Children's Initiative. His stories are also published by Lune Spark. He enjoys reading science fiction, rowing and canoeing.

Javan Dean is a fifteen-year-old author from The Bahamas. He has received a plethora of awards and accolades, including being a published author and famed public speaker. He aspires to be a leader who makes the world a better place.

Bezawit Ayelign Fentahun is a first year university student at Gondar University from the Addis Ababa City Administration, Ethiopia. She is currently in her first year of university education at Gondar University. She was among the top students who had successfully passed the national-level university entry examination. Her academic interest is in law education, in the field of sustainable development law.

Charles Bonney Ghartey is a fifteen-year-old writer from Cape Coast in Ghana who loves art, math, and science. He enjoys coding and works on projects like the 'energy light meter' and Wildlife Fire Alarm, where he combines his interests to create helpful innovations.

Ramez Hammoud is a thirteen-year-old eighth grade student at MAC Islamic School in Edmonton- Canada, who enjoys reading and basketball. A YMCA Counsellor-in-Training graduate, he is fluent in English, French, and Arabic. Passionate about environmental conservation, Ramez aspires to become a lawyer, work as a camp counsellor, and advocate for community change.

Rayshal Tharun Harshal is a promising student at DPS Sharjah. Currently in sixth grade, she balances academics with writing, public speaking, and sports. Recently named the youngest all-rounder in her grade, Rayshal's diverse talents, compassion and love for planet Earth makes her a dedicated SDG Ambassador.

Sophia Jalkh is a second-year Environmental Health student studying at the American University of Beirut in Lebanon, minoring in political science. She studies the inter-section of politics and the environment, which she believes to be the primary conflict in the world today. She won first place twice in the Model United Nations (MUN) at the Lebanese American University Global Classroom MUN, and has been a trainer for the program for the last two years.

Rosie James is a thirteen-year-old writer from Coromandel, New Zealand. She is homeschooled on a coastal farm in Te Kouma.. She loves to draw, swim, read, snorkel, play inline hockey and do lapidary and woodwork with her grandfather. Her favourite subjects are sports, art, reading and writing.

Mahnoor Jamshaid is a thirteen-year-old student at PakTurk Maarif School in Islamabad, Pakistan. She comes from a Muslim family and loves to read and write.

Naomi Kene is a thirteen-year old writer from Ontario, Canada who has a passion for art, enjoys reading, and writing fantasy, murder mystery, and thriller stories. Over the past few years, she has enjoyed exploring her creativity through writing and drawing. Her enthusiasm for storytelling and drawing brings joy to her friends and family.

Myat Pan Khit is a passionate youth advocate from Myanmar and member of UNICEF EAPRO's Young People's Action Team. Outside of volunteering and teaching, she enjoys reading books and listening to music. Inspired by her mother, Sandar, her story aims to inspire youth while she dreams of studying environmental engineering.

Tasnim Lamine is a fifteen-year-old high school student from Morocco. She lives in Dakhla in the south of Morocco. She defends humanitarian issues, human rights, and the environment.

Lily Abibi Malaika Namata is a sixteen-year-old from Malawi, Africa. Driven by her passion for medicine, she hopes to be an oncologist and make a significant difference in the battle against cancer. She aspires for her writing to foster awareness, promote compassion, and inspire transformation within her community. Lily hopes to become a source of inspiration for others, especially young girls, to help show them that they too can break barriers and pursue their dreams.

Ananya Manikandan, recipient of the international Diana Award and Sharjah Award for Educational Excellence from the United Arab Emirates, excels in academics and talents including singing, dancing, creative writing, public speaking, and theatre. Her filmmaking skills have earned awards and international screenings. Her story, "Cherry Blossom" has been featured in Story Cart 3 at the Sharjah International Book Fair.

Shyam Manikandan, a recipient of the international Diana Award, excels in academics and talents including singing, creative writing, public speaking, and theatre. His film-making skills have earned him awards and international screenings, and he was featured in Story Cart 3 for literary achievements at the Sharjah International Book Fair.

Tyra S. Nettey is a seventeen-year-old Liberian student from Bong County, Gbarnga. Her tribe is Kpelleh and she currently lives in Montserrado County. Her ambition is to become a doctor, to be precise an Otolaryngologist. A Christian, she has taken on leadership roles in her church over the years. She is committed to leading her community to a more green and sustainable future.

Khwahish Punjabi is a creative and accomplished student from Delhi Private School Sharjah. She holds various international awards for her poetry and articles and shares her thoughts through speeches and podcasts. She strongly believes that ingenuity is needed to tackle climate change.

Roland Félix Kadoukpè Sotiré Sotouma is a twenty-year-old native Waama writer from Benin. He studied in Savè and then continued his secondary education in Natitingou. Currently he is specializing in plant production at the Natitingou agricultural technical high school. He is involved in various youth organizations and advocates for the Sustainable Development Goals.

Adam Tabesh is a nine-year-old fourth grade student at Lycée Français International Élite in Beirut-Lebanon who enjoys basketball and soccer. Fluent in French, English, and Arabic, he is also learning Spanish and German. He loves reading, painting, and drawing. Passionate about words and numbers, Adam aspires to become a lawyer, advocating for responsible citizenship and environmental protection.

Luna Tabesh is a twelve-year-old seventh grade student at Lycée Français International Élite in Beirut, and enjoys piano, chess, painting, and writing. Fluent in French, English and Arabic, and learning German and Spanish, she masters language slang and public speaking. At ten, she conducted her first interview on International Women's Day, championing justice, fairness, and human dignity.

Tasheni Gladys Tembo is a sixteen-year-old from Lusaka, Zambia. She is in eleventh grade at Roma Girls Secondary School, Lusaka, and she enjoys natural sciences. Her interests are reading, writing, and creative designs. She aspires to be a specialist doctor in neurosurgery.

Varnessa Kayen Varlyngton is a passionate thirteen-year-old environmental activist from Nigeria. As a young climate advocate, writer, Indigenous environmental journalist, UNICEF Nigeria young influencer, RippLED Fellow, Kidprenuer Ambassador and animator, she is dedicated to raising awareness about environmental justice and children's rights. She is also a Research Scholar at the prestigious Girls in Research program, a volunteer at UNESCO YOD, and the founder of Egalitarianism for Earth.

Tahani Moosa Wadiwala is a passionate and driven sixteen-year-old from Johannesburg, South Africa. She draws inspiration from her mother's dedication to climate advocacy. Her parents instilled in her a deep sense of responsibility towards the planet. Empowered by her family's unwavering support, she hopes to make a meaningful impact and ignite change through her words.

Mohammed Al Zayegh is a seventeen-year-old eleventh grade student living in Gaza -Palestine. He is interested in reading and writing. His hobbies are playing football and swimming. Throughout his years at school, he participated in many competitions in different fields, such as academics and sports and one day he hopes to be a doctor.

The Daughter of the Earth

Varnessa Kayen Varlyngton, Nigeria

Grandmother Sarima approached her granddaughter, Princess Nyeche, who sat by the river, troubled by the weight of the world on her shoulders. As she took a seat beside Nyeche, she asked, "Child, why do you worry?"

Nyeche looked at her grandmother with a mix of determination and sadness. "Mama, they say we incur the wrath of the gods, but is it not our own actions that bring suffering to our land? How can they blame the gods for our misdeeds?" The chirping of birds ceased, and the wind stilled. "My daughter, why do you think so much?" Grandmother Sarima asked, concerned.

Nyeche's eyes became cloudy as she spoke, "They say we anger the gods and they punish our land... But is that really true? Aren't we the source of all our problems? How can they be so blind to their actions yet blame it on the gods of our land."

"Look at the people of the east, take a look at the city of the west, Mama," Nyeche continued, her voice filled with emotion. "Have you forgotten the soot crisis that affected coastal areas in the south too? Even the people of the North, yet no one is speaking out for our rights. How can I stay silent in the midst of chaos? How can I, Princess Nyeche, daughter of the Eze, stay silent when the people of Rivers suffer from environmental injustice? They find no peace, Mama... No peace at all."

Grandmother Sarima listened intently, her gentle movements reflecting the moonlight. "What kind of world do you wish to live in?" she asked.

"I wish for a world where everyone's future is secure and nature is blooming," Nyeche said with determination. "A world where true love lies on majestic isles."

Mama looked at her with a knowing smile. "This is all in your imagination. Why don't you go out there and make that change?"

As she spoke, the moonlight seemed to shimmer with a magical glow, infusing the princess with a sense of purpose and determination. Nyeche, feeling empowered, stood up and moved into the river, bathing herself to ease her boiling pain and despair. Later, as Nyeche returned to the palace, she overheard a scream coming from the western side of the forest. Alert and prepared, she picked up her bow and arrow and ventured into the dense, dark forest.

Following a mysterious trail of glowing fireflies, she felt an inexplicable pull, as if they were beckoning her to follow. They led her to a clearing where she encountered the forest spirit, a being of ethereal beauty and wisdom. The spirit urged her to look into the mirror and see what lay beyond the surface. Intrigued and a little apprehensive, she gazed into the pool, and as she did, the water seemed to ripple and shift, revealing a vision of a world unlike anything she had ever seen. It was a world of vibrant colours and breath-taking landscapes, a place that seemed to exist beyond the boundaries of her own reality.

The forest spirit whispered softly, "Follow me, and I'll show you the way." And with that, she had stepped into the mirror, crossing over into a realm of magic and wonder that lay hidden within the heart of the forest.

Nyeche entered and felt her body weaken and stiffen, she could not move any part of her body and even talk, all she could do was watch. Starting from the beginning of creation where earth was filled with wonder. Nyeche looked closely with awe as the forest spirit sang an ancient song that amplified the cries of mother nature, especially those of the sea creatures who yearn for human understanding. The water moved majestically but its movement demonstrated a hint of sadness. The wind curled around her making her realize that they were family as she felt a surge of warmth and connection with the creatures.

"This is my home," Nyeche confirmed with tears in her eyes.

Nyeche woke up with her heart heavy with dread, her body now dry as she lay on the bed. She opened her eyes and was startled. Grandmother Sarima walked up to her and asked her "why did you swim deep into the water and catch a cold? We found you on the soil, unconscious." The princess was surprised, how is that possible? Clearly, she was at the forest spirit's mirror.

"Grandmother, may I speak to King Father?" Nyeche asked with a new aura.

At the royal court, she approached her father, the king, and the gathered village chiefs. "Mother Nature is in conflict, and we must act swiftly," she urged.

"I communed with the spirits of the forest," she continued, her words carrying a weight of solemnity. "They lament how we exploit and disregard them, treating them as if they were expendable. These creatures, cherished by nature, suffer at our hands. We have abandoned our role as caretakers, forgetting that family extends beyond blood to encompass all life. Why do we inflict harm when we should protect?"

Her impassioned plea was met with murmurs of dissent among the elders, accusing her of opportunism and resource-seeking.

Enraged, the king strode towards her, his face etched with anger. He seized her arm, his voice laced with frustration. "Enough of this folly! If you persist in this reckless talk, I will strip you of your title and banish you!"

"I care not for titles!" she retorted defiantly. "I only seek to be heard. What use is being a princess if my voice is silenced?"

With that, she turned and fled into the shadows, leaving behind a stunned silence in the hall.

As she strolled into the forest, she fell by a pond and cried deeply. "The elders don't care, they don't believe in me, and now lots of things are happening. I just wish for a world where we as humans value our planet. I just wish for a planet where we as humans value nature and live in harmony with the environment, preserving its beauty and resources for future generations. It's heart-breaking to witness the destruction and disregard for the natural world, and the impact it has on the delicate balance of ecosystems. I long for a world where the cries of the earth are heard and heeded, where we come together to protect and nurture the planet that sustains us." Tear drops streamed from her eyes.

It felt like the wind began to speak to her, a melody erupted around her, saying, "Mahatma Gandhi said, 'You must be the change you wish to see in the world.'" She got up, scared, and looked around but saw no one there.

"Recently, it's as if the earth chose me to be. It's calling me and pleading. I cannot fail, even just this time I cannot!"

Just one girl, one world.

But this is not the end of the story; it is the beginning of one...

As she stood by the pond, feeling the weight of the earth's call, she made a silent vow to herself and to the planet. She knew that she could not ignore the urgency she felt to make a difference.

With newfound determination, she set out on a journey to learn more about environmental conservation and sustainable living. She sought out like-minded individuals and joined local environmental groups, where she found a community of people who shared her passion for protecting the planet. Together, they organized clean-up efforts, tree planting initiatives, and educational workshops to raise awareness about the importance of preserving nature.

As she became more involved in environmental activism, her voice grew stronger, and she found herself speaking out on behalf of the earth at community events and gatherings. Her message of valuing nature and living in harmony with the environment resonated with many, and she inspired others to join her in the fight to protect the planet.

Through her dedication and unwavering commitment, she became a beacon of hope for her community and beyond. Her efforts not only made a tangible impact on the local environment but also inspired a global movement towards sustainability and conservation.

The news spread like a wildfire. Everyone became determined to build a sustainable and friendly environment, protecting mother nature. The Eze was deeply impressed with his daughter, at the same time filled with guilt. He sent his orders to call Nyeche to restore her title as a princess "She's not just Princess Nyeche of her kingdom, but the Princess of Nature," he said.

On hearing the news, Nyeche was filled with excitement and did not hesitate to go back home, not because of the title but because she missed her family - she missed home. Everyone rejoiced when she arrived and she was surprised yet grateful for the tender warmth and love shown by them. Finally, when the crown touched her head she said "I am Princess Nyeche, The daughter of the Earth, Nature's Guardian."

And as they watched the majestical sunset, Princess Nyeche spoke in a calm tone filled with ambition "Toast to a more sustainable future!"

The Cure of Mamamia

Luna Tabesh, Canada, Adam Tabesh, Lebanon, and Ramez Hammoud, Lebanon

Once upon a time in the galaxy playground, there was a rocky planet called Mamamia. The atmosphere of Mamamia enveloped her like a blanket. This blanket was knotted with two close ties, superhero friends called NITRO for Nitrogen and OXY for Oxygen. They teamed up to make us breathe and be alive, full of energy.

Mamamia used to be bright and colourful like a beautiful garden, but lately, she had been feeling very sick with a hot fever. Her cosmic blanket was getting messy, dirty, and polluted.

Mamamia needed help, so she called her celestial buddies in the cosmos and asked for a meeting. She wanted to share her feelings with them in hopes they could find a cure soon. They all welcomed her call because they were feeling the same way.

Sola the Sun was tired and exhausted because she was always busy and active, which made her feel hyperactive lately. Luna the Moon looked blurred and hazy. Zen the Stars felt dim. Canopy the Sky felt sad and depressed about her brownish and smoggy appearance. Pufferetti the Clouds felt suffocated. The rain was stuck. Roar the Thunder was angry. Aqua the Oceans were distressed because of the warming water. Woody the Forest, where little trees felt weak and old trees felt ashamed. Sola and Luna asked if the meeting could be held in the afternoon so they could be closer and have a bit of time to meet, even though they sat far apart.

Woody the Forest apologized for not being able to attend the meeting because the young trees did not understand the problem, and the old trees had no leaves to wear. But Woody suggested inviting Guardian, the human being, to the meeting because humans should listen and understand the situation and the risks of not taking the right measures to solve the problems.

Her suggestion was accepted.

The meeting was scheduled one afternoon in spring, with Guardian present. He appeared arrogant, still wearing a shield because he felt guilty. All invitees arrived on time, ready to speak out, listen, and think.
Mamamia started the meeting with an anxious voice: "Friends, thank you all for agreeing to meet as one team. That's why we call ourselves family and friends. As you know, we are all in trouble! We don't feel good. We're facing an enemy that we need to face together. Otherwise, we might all be in danger. Once, we lived and worked

peacefully. Everyone had their own job and schedule. We managed our time in this cosmos without any problems. But because of careless acts, neglect, and selfishness from humans, all life is now at risk.

We need to talk and think together to find the best solution for all of us. Let's plan to save our lives and the environment so we can all live happily and in peace. This is very important for the future of humanity."

Sola asked for permission to speak first as she had to leave soon. She was shining, enthusiastic, full of energy, and spoke loudly: "Thank you, Mamamia, for calling this very important meeting. As you said, we are friends and family, and we all need to come together to face this life challenge. Unfortunately, global warming is causing me trouble. Very often, my temperature is high, and it becomes hard for me to control it. I am sure this affects you and all our friends and family members in the cosmos. But as you know, it's not my mistake; I'm just doing my job. Also, these days, things are getting worse. I'm afraid I won't be able to deal with it anymore in the future. I believe I can only manage it if we all join forces to help me".

Luna, appearing blurry and hazy, said in a faint voice: "I feel diffused and obscured. My visibility is reduced, and I often feel useless as it becomes difficult to shine my light at night."

Zen, flickering faintly, intervened: "We are all feeling dim because of the pollution. It's hard to shine through all the haze of the carbon in the ozone layer."

Canopy, who looked weary and pale, sighed deeply. Mamamia, feeling pity for her, asked for her thoughts. Canopy said, "Mamamia, you know me very well. Do you remember my old beauty? My colour was always bright, clear, and blue. Unfortunately, these days I've become brownish and grey. I'm exhausted from the pollution. This also affects the colour of the oceans and seas. Have we ever looked like this? You tell me!"

Mamamia said, "Not at all dear Canopy. You have always represented to us creativity, imagination, and big dreams. Your bright blue colour reflects cleanliness, positivity, and the majesty of nature. Stay powerful and strong; we will find the solution, no worries."

Pufferetti, who was listening carefully, coughed because she felt suffocated with rain.

Mamamia asked her to calm down and speak slowly. Pufferetti said, "I am carrying a large amount of water, and sometimes it leaks as I lose control. I don't have enough space to handle it anymore. I feel the disturbance that affects Guardian and the agricultural calendar many times during the year, as well as the animals and insects. I believe… (coughs)… it's time to rain when needed and have some rest sometimes to get ready for winter. It's hard to take a vacation."

Aqua intervened, saying, "Absolutely, I'm filled with trash and garbage. Plastic bottles and bags are invading my waters, and my fish friends are suffering. It becomes hard for them to swim and find food, and it hurts their homes."

Mamamia, feeling empathetic, said, "Thank you, everyone, for sharing your thoughts. It's clear that we all feel uncomfortable. We need to find out why this is happening so we can suggest the best ways to help ourselves."

Canopy said, "We all know that pollution is destroying us. Guardian is involved in deforestation, using non-renewable resources, not recycling, and using chemicals and pesticides, among many other irresponsible things."

Here, Guardian, who had entered the meeting looking arrogant, proud, and confident at first, was now calm, with his eyes downcast. He felt guilty about what had been said. He held his hand over his head, trying to find a solution.

Mamamia looked at him with a serious gaze and said, "Guardian, we owe your presence to Woody, who unfortunately couldn't be here today, but she suggested your name to join our meeting. What do you think about what you heard today?"

Guardian, feeling ashamed, mumbled, "Mamamia, yes, I heard what was said, and I feel deeply sorry for what I heard today. I didn't know that the situation was so dire. Today, I realized the level of responsibility we hold and the pain we have caused to all of you and to us as human beings. Even though you all work for us—for our benefit, happiness, security, and safety—"

Mamamia, I am glad that you listened to us carefully, and you now understand the urgency to resolve these problems. My question for you is, how do you think we can overcome these challenges?"

Guardian said, "As you know, we have worked on setting the SDGs, the seventeen Sustainable Development Goals, that should be attained by 2030. I believe we should work hard from now on to achieve them, without rest."

Mamamia nodded sadly, "Then, what would be your plan?"

Guardian said, "We should start by teaching others and spreading the word about how to take care of all of you. I'll tell everyone what I heard today from you. It all starts with each of us, but I need your help to be practical. Can you tell me what worries you the most and how we can fix it?"

Sola, still feeling warm but now focused, suggested, "I want you to use more renewable energy like solar power, so you will rely less on burning fossil fuels. Then, you can harness my energy in a way that does not harm Mamamia."

Luna, feeling hopeful, added, "Please save energy at night and turn off unnecessary lights. This will help me shine brighter and keep the tides steady."
Pufferetti, feeling a bit relieved, said, "I can hold water better if you use systems that save water, plant more trees, and stop cutting them to keep the weather stable."

Canopy said, "Speaking on behalf of Woody, I second that reforestation is important. Trees help absorb carbon dioxide and give us oxygen. Also, they will help you to reduce carbon emissions and make the air cleaner."

Aqua added, "I personally call for reducing plastic waste, stopping overfishing, and using sustainable fishing practices that are crucial to my well-being."

Mamamia said with a caring voice, "Guardian, as Mother Earth, I know we need the voices of all women and mothers everywhere. They make a big difference because they take care of our planet like they take care of their families."

Guardian replied, "Absolutely, Mamamia, it starts with them. We, as Guardians, need to join efforts to make this change. I promise we will meet again in 2030 with a new, clean, and well-organized world."

The meeting concluded, and all promises were documented. They agreed to reconvene in 2030.

Communities around the world noticed changes. Solar panels were installed, trees were planted, oceans were cleaned, and the air became clearer. It all began with education and awareness. Mothers played a crucial role in teaching the right things, so people were inspired by the stars' message and worked together to protect their planet.

As the years passed, Mamamia became fresh, smiling, and happy, living in peace. She had seen significant improvements: renewable energy had become the norm; reforestation had flourished with Woody now filled with adolescent and adult trees that were fresh and green. Fruits and vegetables were organic and edible, and Canopy was clean and clear as pollution levels dropped dramatically.

Mamamia received a call from Guardian inviting her to a meeting with all cosmic friends and family to celebrate the Guardians' achievements. Since it was a night-time event, Sola apologized for not attending but sent her greetings to everyone. She expressed gratitude and happiness for the remarkable achievement made in a short time. Sola asked Guardian to convey that with the help of the Guardians, she successfully spread her power softly and calmly, and now solar energy was powering cities everywhere. Sola felt happy and proud.

Luna added, "I agree. By saving energy at night, I can glow softly and improve visibility for all species. There's no more obscurity, and tides remain stable."

Zen, shining brilliantly, chimed in, "Absolutely! As pollution has decreased, we are visible to everyone again, reminding them of the beauty of night."
Pufferetti, feeling light and free, said, "I feel freedom now. Rainfall is more predictable, and water systems are sustainable."

Guardian, feeling proud but humble about these achievements, smiled and thanked everyone, saying, "We've shown that with determination and cooperation, we can overcome any challenge. Our planet is healthier and more vibrant because of our efforts."

The Echoes of Seascapes

Khwahish Punjabi, United Arab Emirates

It took the sharp peck of Jalal for the juvenile boy to rouse from his realm of imagination. "You naughty falcon! I always wonder how Jaddi was so tolerant with you." exclaimed Faras, in a tone imitating a feeling of annoyance.

For the first few minutes, Faras familiarized himself with his surroundings. Blank canvases stacked up like the Leaning Tower of Pisa, the atmosphere carrying the faint trace of acrylic paint. Brushes lay on the desk which his head was rested on, and there were vivid splashes of colour all over the palms of his hands. Next to him was an old man, who had bushy, salt-and-pepper eyebrows and moustache, a pair of camel brown eyes, and a colourful smile.

That is how every morning went when young Faras woke up in Jaddi's art studio. Jaddi's warm smile would be the first thing he would find when waking up, except now it was framed in glass, and it would remain like that forever.

Jaddi was Faras' favorite person, the one who prepared the canvases for Faras' wonderful and passionate art. He taught him how to paint unique strokes of his creativity, splashes of colours, and unravel his masterpieces to the eyes of others. That is how Faras developed the driving force for his artistic skill. However, things were not the same after Jaddi left for the Almighty's realm. Faras still aspired to work relentlessly but now he felt something was missing from his art. Faras still aspired to work relentlessly as well as attain out of his ability, and he needed to proceed on it as soon as he could.

But now was not the moment to ponder such questions, for he had to think of a way to face his mother's scoldings. "What should I do Jalal? Ummi is not going to let me return here if she figures out that I spent the dusk here once again,'" he asked, only receiving Jalal's look of disapproval and his feathered wings flapping away. Faras sighed, as he took off his paint-covered apron and washed his hands in the stained wash basin. He cleared his throat and trained his insistent tone a couple times to get his mother to excuse him.

As he rushed into the house from the art studio, his mother stood with a stern and intimidating glare. Faras gulped his saliva, and quietly approached her. "Slept over at the 'art haven' of yours again? How many times have I told you to return before the sun sets to rest?!," his mother scolded, "From now on, you will not be permitted to go to the art studio," he replied in mustering all the courage he could when facing such and imposing figure, "Yaa Ummi, please let me go! I promise it will not happen again. I am working on a big project, and it is going to be my masterpiece! Please let me go!" Faras pleaded.

"Faras, you've been talking about this 'masterpiece' for over five years. Either way, this is the final warning, back at home before the sunset or else," his mother stated, giving him a chance, although she already sensed Faras' cheeky expression behind his pleading eyes. "Yay! Thanks Ummi, love you!" Faras exclaimed, grabbing the piece of bread that was on his plate, running back to the art studio. "Oh, my little Fannan..." His mother murmured, as she let out a chuckle watching his enthusiastic stride on the trail back.

As he burst through the doors, he was confronted by the huge canvas that stood proudly at the other end of the studio, one of Jaddi's incomplete artworks. "Jaddi always wanted to paint the sea. He always told me about how each wave symbolized each laugh we shared, and merged with the footmarks we left on the wet sand to blend into the emblem of our bond." Faras told himself, as he walked towards the canvas, and then he stopped only a few steps away from it.

"Finishing his incomplete masterpiece will be the core of my masterpiece. I will dedicate this canvas to the sea of our memories, and the special bond of ours." Faras stated confidently, as he looked upon the fresh blue, aspiring to complete the canvas' tale.

Faras decided to lead the adventure in his intrepid charm. "Step one, sneak out to go to the shore!" as his voice echoed through the art studio, but luckily muffled his voice enough so as to not reach his mother's ears. He beckoned towards Jalal, who stood on the timber perch at the corner of the room and signalled him to fly towards the shore.

And so, as Jalal glided across, Faras chased him to the shore. He giggled in thrill, excited to return to marine nostalgia. "Salaam, my dear sea of memories, which brings the blue waves to the coast!" But to Faras' surprise, the sea was not a pompous shade of bright blue anymore, but rather a gloomy one.

"What is this veil across your beauty, my dear ocean? How come Jaddi has never seen this before?" Faras wondered, "And...what are these new additions of hues?" Faras looked closer and noticed the fragments of plastic, the stains of oil, and the intense shades of waste material as he looked across the coast.

Jalal flew across the sea and returned on Faras' shoulder with a disappointed gaze piercing into his eyes. "I understand, Jalal, the sea is different from what she was before, but maybe she is just trying on a new look." Faras told Jalal with a reassuring smile, as he ran his fingers through his feathers. "Alright, since we have explored the muse of our canvas, let's collect the shades, prepare our base, and return home before it turns dark."

"Hmm...so first, we need to tint this blue with a bit of...grey and black?" Faras claimed, sounding a bit puzzled. So, he sat on the ground, mixing the shades and diluting them a bit just to get the right one. And after attaining the right one...SPLASH! The fluid black spilled onto the blue.

As the black splashed onto the canvas, an ominous feeling splashed on Faras' expression. He tried to reassure himself by deceiving his eyes that it did not affect the visual much. However, deep inside the ocean of his thoughts, it did not illuminate the same charm as before. Faras, astonished at his own mood, lost the impulse to continue the artwork. "What is this feeling that has filled me? There's still two hours until sunset..." he mumbled; a bit disappointed. For one of the first times, Faras walked out of the studio, upset, and discouraged.

The next day, Faras woke up at sunrise and put on his kandura, as he snacked on a handful of dates on his way back to the unfinished artwork. With some hope, he wielded the brush and began painting the elements of disguised destruction.

The list of days went by in the month's scroll. And each day, Faras was dissatisfied with the outcome of his progress. "It doesn't seem quite as it was in my imagination...Is it because of the edges? Or the shade of water! Maybe it needs to be darker." Another splash of black onto the canvas rested on the surface, elements drawn and painted over and over, to the point the edges dripped paint, and the canvas became exceedingly wet.

"NO NO NO! This is not turning out the way I want it to! This is not my sea of memories!" Faras cried out of frustration. He could not find any crystal of rejuvenation and nostalgia in the depiction he tried to paint. He splashed more paint, tried to figure out the right hues of each piece, diluted over and over, until... The canvas met its ravaged fate.

Faras' was frightened at the open slit that lay in the focus of the canvas. Tears welled up in his eyes that held optimism all along the journey of working on his 'masterpiece.' "What have I done? I ruined the work of art which incorporated the remaining passion of Jaddi's memories with mine..." He cried aloud.

Jalal watched Faras cry till the sun had set and let out a loud screech to alert him of dusk. Meanwhile, Faras' mother grew worried, and decided to see what her son was up to, only to see her son sobbing uncontrollably, holding the glass frame of his Jaddi. "My son! What's wrong?" she asked out of concern. "Ya Ummi...I ruined the canvas of the sea. This is all my fault! I just wanted to make it look identical to the sea...But I don't know what happened!" Faras yelped.

"It is not your fault, my dear son. The sea is just like your canvas, and the people who have painted it must perceive that it was picturesque by itself. It doesn't require any more elements, nor the brushstrokes. That's what your Jaddi too always wanted to portray through his efforts and art, but time wasn't in his favour. He always told me that one day, you would mature to become nature's 'Fannan,' to paint nature in order to restore its beauty. And I always believed in him, and I believe in you. Faras, repaint the beauty of your muse."

"Now come my son, take some rest." His mother told him, with a supportive smile in the hopes of restoring his confidence. Jalal too, let out a shriek of cheer. Faras did not respond, but his eyes gained their sparkle of possibilities again. That night, Faras laid on his bed, and dreamt about what he had to do next.

Faras followed Jalal back up on the trail towards the shore. But this time Faras didn't arrive to attend the sea with his paint-stained palms, rather holding a bag Jaddi made out of palm leaves to clean up the waste present in the water.

"Mr. Yusuf! I'm borrowing this rowboat, hope it's okay!" Faras asked Yusuf, the dockmaster. "Yes, dear son, go ahead. Have a lovely time at Sea!" Yusuf replied in a tone of encouragement. Faras beamed confidence, as he hopped on the boat and rowed ahead, the waves eager to navigate him.

He gathered up every piece of trash he could see and collected it in the bag. He watched Jalal glide through the sky, taking pride in Faras' actions. People watched in amazement gaining courage to follow them as unbeknownst to him they prepared to come to join him in cleaning up the area they called home. "There is only one chamber that we must persist in. And that is the chamber from which the voyage of our resolutions begins." He shouted out, hearing it loud and clear, and followed by the collective pattering sound through the waves.

Faras turned back to see in amazement every worker at the shore, in rowboats with palm bags. They all yelled and applauded, raising their arms, and waving their hands. Trained divers soon went into the sea, discovering the essence of their culture again for a solution of sustainability. Jalal flapped his wings in the air, cheering them on.

"Let's do this, everyone! Unveil the blue beauty of the sea again!" Faras yelled, leading them on. Everyone worked hard till sunset, and a beautiful panorama was captured. Faras and the team of his supporters had cleaned up nearly all the trash present in the sea near the coast. As everyone rowed back to the shore, Jalal descended back down on Faras' shoulder.

At night, Faras slept, exploring the realm of his dreams to see the azure streak of blue blend with the brown sand again. Almost predicting what would soon happen, his dreams would come true.
"FARAS! FARAS! Wake up, son!" His mother excitedly exclaimed, shaking him lightly. "Ummi, what...happened?" Faras asked, in a sleepy tone. "My dear son, your voice has echoed to other citizens across the country. They have seen your determination in achieving clean oceans and seas and are willing to be a contributor to restoring the bright azure gem!" His mother explained. Faras' sleepy eyes widened in surprise, and jubilation overtook him. "My sea of memories, I can't wait to see you again!" He yelled, jumping off his bed and hugging his mother.

Faras continued to work to clean the sea by organizing clean-up drives amongst his community, and people eagerly took part in it. Indeed, he could see the gradient transition from the gloomy, grey-tinted blue to a recovering azure. He also went back to his 'art haven' and renewed the canvas project of his. This time, he coated his base with the rich shade of nostalgia indigo, the waves of change, and used the earth's shades to instil the significance of moments into his artwork. His palms found its paint stains again, his fingers found the power to wield the paintbrushes, and his heart found its way to follow his passion again.

A few weeks later, Faras was applying the final additions to his masterpiece, until an enthusiastic Jalal came to the window, flapping his wings in excitement. "What's gotten you so excited Jalal- HEY! That's Jaddi's picture frame! Where do you think you're going with it?!" Jalal picked up the picture frame and flew out the window. Faras quickly tracked after Jalal on the ground.

His chasing feet felt the texture of sand, as Faras found himself at the shore again. Jalal rested his claws on the ground, as he carefully placed the glass frame. Then, he took flight just to grab the canvas from Faras' embrace and hold it up.

To Faras' amazement, he saw a crystal resemblance of his masterpiece with the azure sea that had been cleaned up and unveiled from its cloak of destruction. The waters reflected the warm shades of sunset, embraced flashes of the past, and carried memories in each wave.

The young boy sat down next to the glass frame of his Jaddi and took it in his arms. "Yaa Jaddi...how I wish you were to see me and be my guiding light, as I follow in your footsteps of bringing change." He spoke, looking into the eyes of his Jaddi's picture. "I can't thank you enough for this! I'm so grateful that you're the reason for my passion, my actions, my courage and my potential."—SCREECH! A discontented Jalal let out a screech, pecking Faras mischievously, as Faras laughed. "And the reason Jalal is here with me," he said.

And so, the three of them sat to watch the sunset at shore. Jaddi, framed as the guiding light of passion and dedication; Jalal, the emblem of pride and superiority; and finally, Faras, bearing his canvas of depiction, symbolized the beacon of change, the sea's saviour, and the painter of restoration.

"You know, Jaddi, I now realize what you told me. It takes determination to yield the brush in order to find hope in each stroke, recover harmony with each shade, and blend the simple colours to reinstate Nature's peace. That is indeed the real essence of Nature's Fannan." Faras spoke, letting his gaze fall at his smile, and back at the jewel of azure beauty.

Tradition and Innovation Unite

Roland Félix Kadoukpč Sotiré Sotouma, Benin

Nestled amidst the lush mountains of Benin, in the heart of Natitingou, lies the village of Pouya, where a tale of ancestral tradition meeting scientific progress, environmental protection clashing with economic aspirations, unfolded.

Nahini, the village's elder sage, guardian of ancestral knowledge and protector of the land, watched with concern as changes swept around him. The forest, a source of life and wisdom for generations, was succumbing to the devastating onslaught of logging and intensive agriculture. The Forest Spirits, messengers of climatic upheavals, conveyed alarming visions to him: persistent droughts, devastating floods, and unpredictable storms threatened the fragile balance of the community.

Sotiré, a hopeful young scientist, returned to the village after years of studying in the city. Determined to put his knowledge to the service of his community, he turned his attention to the region's abundant natural resources. He envisioned innovative solutions to harness solar energy and develop sustainable agricultural techniques, all while preserving the rich biodiversity.

Nekima, a courageous mother, shared the concerns of Nahini and Sotiré. Torn between the need to provide for her family and protect the environment, she felt powerless in the face of the immense challenges. Deforestation was depriving her village of the natural resources she depended on to feed her children and secure their future.

Konté, a curious and intelligent young boy, fascinated by nature and technology, listened attentively to the adults' discussions. He dreamed of a world where humans lived in harmony with nature, where science and tradition would combine to create a sustainable future.
Sékou, the village's corrupt and powerful chief, reluctant to change, favored immediate and lucrative solutions. He saw the exploitation of natural resources as an opportunity for economic development, without regard for the long-term environmental consequences.
The mayor of the municipality of Natitingou, a politician committed to achieving the Sustainable Development Goals, learned about the villagers' concerns and the solutions proposed by Sotiré. He understood that a balance needed to be struck between economic progress and environmental protection.

One day, Nahini summoned Sotiré, Nekima, Konté, and Sékou for a meeting in the sacred forest. Under the shade of ancient trees, he conveyed the message of the Forest

Spirits: "Ti tingou yiriba wintoman dén bo nan ba non mingin né dé ba ta soki ba basi ban pisi nan winroun sa ba hossi na ba biti ra ba manssi." In English this means that the community's future depended on their ability to unite their forces and find sustainable solutions.

Sotiré presented his sustainable development ideas, explaining how harnessing renewable energy and environmentally friendly agricultural techniques could ensure the village's prosperity while preserving nature. Nekima shared her experiences and observations, highlighting the impact of deforestation on families' livelihoods, and happiness. Konté, with his enthusiasm and curiosity, proposed innovative solutions using technology to monitor forest health and optimize natural resource utilization.

Sékou, initially reluctant, was challenged by the passion and determination of the youth. He understood that sustainable development was not incompatible with economic prosperity, but required a long-term vision and collaboration among all community stakeholders.

Inspired by Nahini's words and united by a common goal, the villagers of Pouya embarked on a new chapter in their history. Led by Sotiré and with the support of the mayor, they developed sustainable agriculture, responsible forestry, and renewable energy projects. Konté, with his talent for technology, created forest monitoring systems and digital tools to optimize natural resource management.

Nekima, regaining hope, was able to provide for her family while contributing to environmental protection. She passed on her knowledge to other women in the village, encouraging them to adopt sustainable agricultural practices and educate their children about the importance of nature conservation. Sékou, recognizing the importance of balancing economic development with environmental protection, advocated for sustainable projects with the authorities. Pouya's transformation did not happen overnight. Heated meetings, passionate debates, and moments of doubt marked the community's journey. But the determination of the villagers, guided by Nahini's wisdom, Sotiré's ingenuity, Nekima's courage, Konté's enthusiasm, and the mayor's will, eventually bore fruit. Fields once devastated by intensive agriculture were transformed into havens of greenery. Villagers adopted agro-ecological techniques, favoring crop rotation, the use of natural compost, and biological pest control. The more abundant and healthier harvests now nourished the entire community, ensuring food security and generating surpluses for sale in local markets.

Uncontrolled logging gave way to sound and sustainable management thanks to the villagers' efforts. Trees, selectively felled and meticulously replanted, continued to offer their precious resources to the villagers while preserving the forest's biodiversity and ecological balance. Forest products harvested in respect of natural cycles, fueled local crafts and provided eco-friendly construction materials. Solar panels, installed on the roofs of houses and community buildings, harnessed the sun's power to provide the village with clean and renewable electricity. This new energy source allowed the abandonment of polluting diesel generators, improving air quality and significantly reducing the community's energy costs. Konté, having become a recognized expert in sustainable technologies, put his expertise to the service of environmental protection. He developed forest monitoring systems, enabling villagers to track the health of trees in real time and detect potential environmental problems. Mobile applications were also created to raise awareness about the importance of biodiversity conservation and promote sustainable agricultural and forestry practices.

The example of the Waama village of Pouya resonated far beyond the lush mountains surrounding the commune of Natitingou. Neighboring communities, facing the same environmental and economic challenges, came to draw inspiration from the successful experience of Pouya in particular and Natitingou in general. Fruitful exchanges and collaborations were born, fostering the dissemination of sustainable practices and the construction of a more environmentally friendly future.

The story of the Waama village of Pouya is a message of hope for all communities aspiring to sustainable development. It demonstrates that economic progress and environmental protection are not mutually exclusive, but can go hand in hand to create a prosperous and harmonious future. Ancestral wisdom, scientific ingenuity, individual courage, and collective will are the keys to a sustainable transformation, serving present and future generations.

The Doves and the Crickets

Javan Dean, The Bahamas

Her name is Danielle Matthews. She lives on a beautiful island in The Bahamas, where her father, Aaron Matthews is the Prime Minister. Each morning, she would rise from her bed and gaze out at the tropical surroundings from her hilltop balcony. This is truly the land of sun, sand and sea. Where she lives is an exclusive area known as 'The Cove'. It is like a bubble where everything is just better—a place where contamination never reaches. She could smell the chicken souse, her favourite Bahamian dish of boiled chicken pieces, root vegetables and spices, brewing downstairs.

"Ms. Danielle, it's time to get ready for the day," the day maid calls. Yes, today is very important. It is the start of a new school year and the first time that students outside of the Cove would be attending. Danielle attended Chesapeake High School, and she loved it there and this year, she was assigned the task of showing the new students around.

As she got ready for school, she gazed out the window beyond the gate that separated the Cove from others. Danielle had the worst bedroom. Beyond the gate, she could catch glimpses of the swampy flooded village called 'The Pond'. She could almost smell the misery from where she stood. How could they get up each day just to work, eat, sleep, and repeat? A sorrowful cycle of dead dreams. "Well, that's none of my concern," she thought and hurried to get ready.

"Good morning, Mother!" she said as she floated down the stairs. Her mom embraced her for a while before pinching her cheeks and saying, "Oh dear you are so beautiful." Her father chimed in that she got her looks from him. They all chuckled together, joining Dad at the breakfast table. Her sister Nicole soon flounced downstairs - the epitome of beauty and superiority. She looked nothing like Danielle, who was adopted, though no one outside the family knew. Danielle's mother always looks at her with a face of anger, she had never really understood why. But it does not matter, her father and sister loved her to death. They shared their delicious breakfast, eating as if there was no tomorrow, and then departed for school.

On the other side of the gates lived Terrance. "Another beautiful day in the pond," he thought sarcastically, slapping the radio with the loud alarm to the ground in frustration. "Terrance, get the hell up!" his mother hollered from the next room. "I gotta be at work fa seven, and you're already late!"

His mother, Ariane, was a housekeeper at the Renaissance Hotel, behind the gates of the Cove. She was a single mother, but never complained about it. Terrance followed her command and used the bucket of water from the public pump to freshen up. Afterwards, he joined his mother and his sister Terranique in the living room for a quick bite to eat. It was pig feet souse yet again, just his luck!

As he sat, he met his mother questioning Terranique about the beautiful dress made with the finest Androsian fabric. Androsian fabric was a handmade cotton material produced and patterned at the Cove. "Where did you get that from?" Ariane asked again, after being met with silence. "Oh, I found it at the thrift store," Terranique said quietly while putting on her coat. The truth was that Terranique was "dating" a rich boy in the Cove. He had gifted her the dress and she could not wait to meet up with him and show off the dress on the first day at Chesapeake High School.

Both Terrance and his sister were on scholarships to attend Chesapeake High School and Terrance prayed that Terranique's prior relationship with the rich boy would not mess that up. "They already don't like us pond folk in their schools," he thought, before rushing out the door to the bus stop. To reach the bus, his sister was walking on her tip-toes, so as to not get her dress wet. The Pond is filled with water, hence the name. The constant flooding was due to the rising sea level. Their tropical island was slowly sinking, that is why all the rich and powerful live on the hill and families like Terrance's live far below them. Every single day, somewhere became an underwater paradise. Homes sinking in the ocean never to be seen again.

The jitney soon came and everyone piled in like a can of sardines. Terrance quickly grabbed a window seat, so he could enjoy the view outside. The transition between the pond and the Cove was especially fascinating to him. From leaning and rusting homes with holes in the walls to two and three-story pearl white mansions with chimneys and gardens, lined up so beautifully as if they were taking attendance. Then came the colossal building that was Chesapeake High School, with a big beautiful fountain at the front.

To Terrance's surprise, his sister stopped the bus just before it neared the school. She then started to head for the side entrance, where nobody entered. Before long, Terrance objected: "What do you think you're doing? We just got here, why are you pulling these shenanigans already? Mom is working very hard for us; just wait till I tell her what you're up to!" he shouted, grabbing her hand. "Who do you think you're talking to? Last time, I checked I'm the older sister and I don't want these rich people to know we're from down under!" she argued while pushing Terrance back.

"Are you ashamed of who we are?" Terrance questioned softly. "Who wouldn't be? We're poor people and you know what Cove folk can do to people like us who they think are less than them. They have done it before and I don't want that to be me!" she replied, tearing up. Terrance paused in sympathy before telling her, "Sis, I know how you feel, but you have to understand that this is the life we live and there's nothing we can do about it!" Though Terrance said the words, he did not understand. Why were things the way they were? Why must the poor work to stay poor? The only thing he could do was hug his sister.

Danielle thanked and waved goodbye to the chauffeur, while her sister walked quickly to take a selfie in front of the school's lavish water fountain. When Danielle joined her, Nicole grabbed her hand and started yapping away. "So, are you ready to help the new kids, Dani?"

Danielle looked at her with a wry smile and replied, "I mean, I guess it'll be fun, besides I want to be Class President next year so I think it'll definitely help," To that, Nicole exclaimed, "Why are you trying so hard? You're the daughter of the Prime Minister!" Danielle gave her the side eye before responding joyfully, "You are too, y'know." After, Nicole only rolled her eyes and continued texting on her glitzy cell phone. Just then, from the corner of Danielle's eyes, she saw two individuals she had never seen before. What was really strange was the way they entered the school, from the side gate.

Danielle found it strange because not even the teachers came through that gate. So, she took her sister's free hand and went to investigate. "Dani, this is how people in horror movies die, by being curious. Why don't we just inform security?" Nicole muttered in disgust, as she was dragged forward. Ignoring her resistance, Danielle continued to move towards the strangers, with her sister's arm tucked under hers.

Upon reaching the side entrance, a boy about six feet tall quickly turned around and pushed the girl he was with behind him. He smiled shyly, "Hi, I'm Terrance, and this is my sister Terranique. It's a pleasure to meet you both." he said, putting his hand out to be shaken. He soon retrieved it.

"I'm Danielle and this is Nicole. Your names sound familiar. Oh, that's right, you two are some of the new students, correct? Why don't I give you a tour of our premises?" Terranique moved ahead of her brother and responded "Sure, whatever," while rolling her eyes.

"Cute dress…" Nicole snickered to Danielle as they moved ahead. "Who wears a dress on the first day of school?" Danielle motioned to Nicole that she was too loud, but it was too late.

"Who the hell do you think you're talking about!" Terranique asked angrily. "I'm talking to you, and what about it?" Nicole said defensively. "What's the matter, you aren't used to Androsian clothing? You must be from The Pond."

Now this is where things got interesting. Terranique took down her ponytail and…….

Thirty minutes later, Terrance was on the phone with his mother. "Mom, this is bad. Terranique just punched somebody's child. We've been at this school for fifteen minutes and Terranique punched somebody's child! We didn't even get a chance to walk through Chesapeake's doors yet! Yes… the girl was provoking, but Terranique knows that we don't have the authority, Mom. It started with a punch then it became a full-blown fight. They were both rolling on the floor. I could not believe it! Fights happen often in The Pond but not here, not at the school in the Cove. This can be bad! Get here now, Mom… we need you!" Terrance hung up the school's secretary's phone and sat back down outside the principal's office next to his sister who looked like she was ready for round two. Terrance leaned over with his head in his hands and mumbled, "I can't believe you did this! This is exactly why they don't let us into their school. Mom's gonna be so mad."

After a while, Terranique seemed anxious and got up to go to the bathroom. When she returned, she complained about her stomach hurting. Terrance assured her that their mom was on the way, but Terranique could not leave without seeing her boy-friend, Thomas. She wanted to see his lovely dreads and milk chocolate skin again. She also needed to talk to him immediately. For one, she needed to ask him about the Androsian dress he insisted she wear, making her look like a fool. And two, she need-ed to ask him about not meeting her this morning at the side entrance. Why would he do a thing like that? she thought.

Thank God the office incident had a break, Terranique thought. Everyone was re-leased to class until parents or guardians showed up. Finally, she could look for Thomas. They desperately needed to talk about what they were going to do about the baby. He was the father. At first, she was all for giving up the child, because teenage pregnancy had ruined so many lives in this country including her own mother's. But she had grown to love the life growing inside her and she didn't want to lose it. "I think

I could work something out with him and maybe we can give this parenting thing a try!" she mused.

She texted him and waited in an empty classroom. When Thomas came up and opened the door, she ran into his arms and they started making out. But then, Terranique pushed him off. "Sorry, we can't do this right now, we need to talk." she asserted.

"What do you mean we need to talk? There's only one thing I want to do about now, and it ain't talking," he smirked while unbuttoning his shirt. "Yeah, we need to talk about the consequences of that, mister," she said, rubbing her belly. "I know, don't worry, I already got a guy who's gonna help you get rid of it like we planned," he said, trying to kiss her neck.

"That's enough! I already told you to stop. And I'm keeping the baby," she bravely exclaimed. "What do you mean?" he shouted. "Hold on, don't be raising your voice at me! This is my body and I'm not getting rid of this baby! We're going to raise it and that's final! Terranique said firmly and began walking away. He ran and grabbed her hand and tried to pull her back. She resisted and the next thing she knew was her face being riddled with front and back hand slaps. The last was a punch that sent her flying to the ground and then everything went black.

The door to Mr. Corban's Biology class opened slowly. Danielle peeped in and took in the situation. With tears dripping down her face, she rushed over to kneel before Terranique, still lying on the ground. "Oh Danielle, it's not what it looks like, I swear!" Thomas blurted, trying to button up his shirt.

At that moment, Terrance arrived on the scene. "What's going on here? What's with all the tears?" he asked in confusion. When he saw Thomas buttoning his shirt and Terranique on the floor, he pieced two and two together and suddenly, anger took control.

"What did you do my sister!" he shouted, while pushing Thomas against the wall." "Oh, so Pond Boy got some angst huh?" Thomas snidely remarked.

Just as Terrance drew his hand back in a fist, Danielle interrupted and shouted, "We need to get her to the hospital now! She is bleeding."

At the hospital, the nurse soon came, clutching a file in her hand. "I have some bad news, but I need an adult present," she said. "Well, I'm their mother, do I count?" Ariane shouted, rushing through the door out of breath. They all took our seats close to Terranique, holding each other's hands. "Terranique will be alright, but the baby..., it's gone. My sympathy to your family." The nurse said, leaving the room. Ariane jumped up so hard that her chair fell back. "What is she talking about, huh? You were expecting a baby?" Terranique replied with a soft "yes," and turned her head away to avoid her mother's outraged gaze. She began to softly weep, thinking about her baby, who was conceived with love in the Pond but died in The Cove. Why was life so unfair?

"Was it for that Thomas kid, your boyfriend!" Ariane asked. "They're the same person, but yes..." She replied crying. "What happened, what did they do to my baby!" Ariane screamed falling to the floor. Then she shot up in the air, "I'm gonna take care of this. They Cove folk are gonna pay!" And just like that she took out her phone and went outside the room.

She was furious, to say the least. She had received a call from the school telling her to go to the hospital. She left work early and took a jitney there. Once she arrived, she had learned that her child was hurt by a male student, who got her pregnant and hit her. Her daughter has lost the baby. She growled to herself "The boy that did this has to be made to pay."

She called an old friend. "Hello, Aaron, is that you? I need some help." I spoke. "What's the matter, Ari? Why are you so worked up?" Mr. Matthews replied. "Long story short, Terranique is hurt and I need your help to press charges against the boy responsible; his name is Thomas," She exclaimed. "Sorry, but..." there was a slight pause before he continued, "I can't help you dear. It'll damage my campaign and my reputation." Mr. Matthews answered.

"How can you even say that? You're her father. Don't you think you should act like it, for once in your life!" Ariane shouted. "You better watch your words, miss. I'm a very powerful man and you're just a measly Pond resident." Mr. Matthews replied. "I won't be measly when I go up to parliament and talk about how you gave me two kids, after taking my first one for your then-barren wife," She shot back. "Try me, Ari and see what I can do to you and your little family." He replied aggressively.

"You better think hard and fast about how important your little campaign is, honey,"

Ariane threatened, before she hung up the phone. When people from the Pond have to choose between sinking or swimming, the one thing they would do is swim. They were born for swimming. Swimming was survival and this time was no different.

The Embrace of the River

Ananya Manikandan, United Arab Emirates

It was five thirty a.m. The sun was slowly rising from the peaks of the Western Ghats, spreading its golden rays across South India. River Noyyal, flowing through the village of Orathupalayam, is a major source of drinking water for millions living in the delta districts of Tamil Nadu.

The people of Orathupalayam slowly stirred awake by the gentle chirping of birds. Suddenly, a strong toxic stench spread throughout the riverbanks. Nina woke up coughing. "Oh no! My asthmatic attack has started again!!" Nina's wheezing sounds instantly woke her daughter, Amala. Amala was just ten years old. She rushed to open the window hoping for a draft of fresh air for her mom. Her eyes instinctively fixed on the nearby Noyyal. "Mom, the colour of water has changed. It is purple today!" claimed Amala innocently. By that time, Nina had already inhaled two puffs of her steroid inhaler. "If this also does not work, I will have to go to the doctor's house for an injection." Nina moaned. Amala looked at her mom with worry. Her mum was already gaining weight with frequent steroid injections. All these issues started with the new garment factory which opened a year ago in their area. Everyone in the village was promised a job in the factory and a new township with world class amenities. Nobody was suspicious about the offer and willingly sold their land in which they used to farm for generations. They were offered jobs as promised. Everyone was happy until they realized the beginning of a major disaster. The river Noyyal started changing colours each day as the dye wastes from the factory contaminated the water.

The village started developing a horrible stench from the river and Amala saw with her own eyes' children playing with dead fish in the river. The fishermen, who used to fish in the river, stopped coming all together. Amala asked the old fisherman who used to give her fresh Ayra fish which is known for its high protein and medicinal values, "Uncle, why did you stop fishing in the river?" He replied "The river is not suitable for life. Everything is dead." Amala was shocked. She could not accept what she was hearing. The whole village was worried, but they were not able to find a solution to this crisis.

One day, during school, Amala's classmate, Sana, suddenly started vomiting and collapsed. Her science teacher entered the class, looking visibly upset and informed the headmistress. A classmate called the number for the ambulance. The paramedics arrived and managed to save her. Meanwhile, Sana's parents told everyone that their well water was contaminated with pollutants from the nearby stained river.

Once Amala returned home, she sent a detailed letter to the local newspaper, "Daily Times" explaining this crisis and attached her poem on river pollution and requested the editor to publish.

Oh, my dear,
What do I do?
Once crystal clear,
now shades of blue!
People so immature,
making you impure.
I can't endure,
this torture for a lure.

Two days later, the school headmistress called Amala and asked, "Did you send a letter to Daily Times?". Amala replied, "Yes ma'am". "Good. The editor wants to meet you. You can go with the science teacher." Amala's school was the only school in her village, giving education till grade five. This school is run by a local charity organization that collects donations to manage expenses and gives free education.

Amala and her teacher visited the editor's office that afternoon. As they turned the street, they saw the big signboard written boldly in blue, "Daily Times" with a slogan, "The Voice of Truth" and with a logo of a hand holding a pen high. Her thoughts flew to her headmistress' speech during her assembly, "The pen is mightier than the sword". They entered the small yellow building, climbed a few steps where a peon greeted them. They were ushered into the main office. Around ten people were there, engrossed in their work and did not bother to notice the newcomers. They sat on a worn-out sofa in the editor's room, waiting for the editor. The gentle humming from the air-conditioner and the chillness calmed her. Mixed thoughts rose in Amala's mind, "Will the editor agree to publish my letter? What will happen after that?"

After fifteen minutes of waiting, her thoughts were interrupted by the shrill voice of the editor, "So, you are the girl who wrote the complaint letter?" "Yes sir, I'm Amala", she replied. She noted the editor, now seated at his desk, was a short bald old man with spectacles at the tip of his nose. He started, "Do you know the consequences of spreading rumours? The factory can even file a defamation case against you and get you arrested for this, and the school can also be closed forever." Amala was stunned. The teacher replied feebly, "But sir, the whole village is affected". The editor said, "I need facts. Even if your accusation is true, a poem written by a child will not create any impact on such issues. Better that you get back to your studies than wasting our time." Amala was enraged, "Sir, you have denied a child the opportunity to have her voice heard on such an important issue. By rejecting my letter, you have not only silenced my voice but also sent a message that our concerns are not important, that our generation does not matter".

The teacher soothingly placed her hand on Amala's shoulder, and they left. The editor went pale and instantly instructed his peon to phone the garment factory manager. The editor informed the manager about the letter and that he wants to publish it. He asked what the factory manager had to say about it so that he could make a cover story out of it. The factory manager requested him not to publish the story by telling, "My factory follows all the safety norms before disposing of the waste. Everything in the letter is untrue and I'm sure that my business competitors are provoking the villagers to spoil my reputation." The manager also reminded the editor of all the sponsorships and advertisements the factory gave to the newspaper to prove his goodwill. The editor was then convinced to dissuade the girl from her supposed wrongdoing.

There was absolute silence at her school for the next two days. Suddenly during lunch time, a small fleet of cars lined up in front of the school entrance. All the children ran out of their classes to witness the fleet. The first blue car opened, and a tall man leaped out. Two other men got out from the cars behind with papers in their hands. The three of them entered the headmistress office. Amala and her friends stood outside the room and anxiously listened to their conversation. The men showed all the documents and informed them that they had taken the land on lease from the current owner and warned that the school would be vacated in three months' time. Feeling guilty, Amala rushed into the headmistress room and told with tears in her eyes, "Ma'am, the editor must be behind all this. I am sorry for putting everyone's future at risk by writing this letter." The headmistress assured her by saying, "Dear, never feel guilty for writing the truth".

The villagers soon learnt of what happened. Amala's heart broke when she heard her neighbour's comment, "Look at this foolish girl Amala. Because of her, the school is going to be shut down". She ran to her mom and cried. Nina hugged and consoled her.

Amala was determined and did not lose hope. She called her friends and they decided to start a public campaign to unite all the villagers. But they knew that it would not be easy. Every day after school, they went house to house and explained the science behind river pollution, its complications and the way to combat it. At first, they explained it to the children of the village knowing they could convince their parents.

Week after week, their campaign gained momentum. One fine day, the village chief called them for a meeting. They clarified all his doubts and provided him with all the scientific data they had uncovered. They wanted to host campaigns in the neighbouring villages where the river Noyyal flowed. The village chief helped garner support from the neighbouring villages. They also decided to conduct a petition, hoping they could use this to approach the editor.

They gather six thousand nine hundred and sixty-eight signatures from the people and Amala went to visit the editor's office again. The village chief and her mother accompanied her for support. She handed over the petition to the editor and said, "Kindly look at this petition. The last time we met, you had accused me of false propaganda and wrongdoing, however, every word of what I had said was true. To prove this, I have conducted a campaign and collected over six thousand signatures in the petition. On behalf of them all, I request you to support our campaign." Overwhelmed with emotion, she placed the papers on his desk and ran out of the office, without glancing back, determined not to be shouted at by the immoral editor.

The school children were counting days. On the last day of the third month, the editor visited the headmistress. Amala was also called into her office. Upon seeing the editor, Amala angrily blurted out, "What mistake have I done by just writing the truth? Why have you put all of us into trouble?" The headmistress said, "Amala, calm down. The editor is not like what you think. After you met him, he sent his reporters to the factory to find the truth. He prepared the reports and sent them to the government authority and personally followed up our case with the minister. He also secured our place back."

Amala stood speechless for a minute. After she regained herself, she asked, "But what will happen to the factory?" The editor replied, "The government has already passed the orders to install the zero-discharge system under direct supervision and take steps to clean up the river to reduce the total dissolved solids from the current level of seven thousand five hundred to below three hundred. The government has also assured the villagers of free medical assistance to those affected." The editor finally rose, turned towards Amala, and handed her a chocolate box and applauded her for her brave act.

He assured her that he had allotted a dedicated column in his newspaper for students writing articles on social and environmental issues.

The next day, Amala opened the Daily Times newspaper. Her eyes shone with tears when she saw her poem published in the newspaper and along with a cover story titled, "The Courageous Daughter of Orathupalayam".

The next few months were the best months of Amala's life! She was thrilled to see that changes were occurring in the river. The changes were slow but steady as time passed. After a short period of time, the river was finally crystal clear again. Amala's joy knew no bounds! She was so excited that she went from door to door announcing to everyone that the water was now fresh and clean, and it was safe to drink. Everything returned to regularity now.

Amala felt happy and content, knowing that she could do something to protect her mother Earth!!

Who Says Dirt Doesn't Shine?

Nana Aisha Bello Abdulkadir, Nigeria

❮❮Three months. It's been three whole months since I've seen a spark of light in this village. I mean, it wasn't like we had unlimited light from the beginning but it was a bit better than this.

And now, we've been lightless for a whole three months. Waiting, begging for it to spark so everyone can scream up and down and rejoice in absolute bliss."

"But yet, here we are, waiting for the light to come. Forced to sit and watch like sheep. All because we ourselves cannot do anything about it. We have to wait for the government to realize we don't have light so they can supply some to us. But can we tell ourselves the truth for just a split second? With the entirety of Nigeria, who's going to care if a small village like ours doesn't have any light when there are so many bigger fish to fry?"

"They're not going to help us. We have to help ourselves. Because whether we like it or not, it is we who are affected the most at the end of the day. So will we just sit idle and wait for the so-called government to supply us with electricity or will we get up, dust off our asses and go do something about it?"

"Look, crazy Mira is back to her old antics again."

"Some things in this village will never change."

"I feel bad for her parents, raising such a menace to society."

What else did she think would be the response when a girl comes out in the middle of the scorching sun to preach about finding renewable sources of electricity? She has been saying the same thing over and over again for the last three months, just praying someone in their small village would care about what she was saying. But alas, her saliva would run dry, her feet tired and body aching at the end of each day. Retiring home to pretend this lack of electricity doesn't bother her.

Mira sighs, packing up her plate and heading towards the kitchen to wash them. She starts to resonate on her ideas, her plans for a better tomorrow. A tomorrow where her people did not have to rely on someone to supply them with electricity. There could possibly be a way for them to make their own light that would never extinguish. Even though she comes up with these ideas in her head, her heart is still telling her that her people would not care about her silly little ambition. As usual, they would call her crazy and insane. As usual, they would jab insults at her. As usual, she would cry herself to sleep, knowing there was nothing she could do about it.

As she packed up the remaining scraps on her dish, she went out to go pour it in the trash can, only to realize the can was full. Before her mother could come and ask her to do it, she quickly got her hijab and gathered the rubbish together. She would make the trip to the village's dump herself. The dump was just an empty land where everyone came to throw out their garbage. It had gathered so much filth that the stench could be recognized by tourists.

And all of it just sitting on a random plot of land with absolutely no supervision whatso-ever. In fact, it was so bad, wild animals have been caught numerous times searching for food to eat and things to build shelters from. It was so bad that it was funny how so many people could just blindly let something like this happen in a village they live in all the time. The trash disposal system in this village was as horrible as it could ever get. It was sickening, to say the very least.

As she threw out the trash, an idea came to her mind. Almost like a little light bulb sparking up in her brain. She grinned to herself, packing up some trash in the bin and taking it home with her. She thought of a way to actually make electricity for the whole village that might actually work. And a way to make people stop dumping their refuge on the ground and causing the place to smell. It was like a hammer hit to the skull when it came to her. Almost a revelation.

She got together some trash, some wires and metal bits and bobs. She put all the trash into a burning fire to make it into charcoal before using the hot charcoals as a renewable means of electricity. Of course, this did not take her one day. The first time she tried it, it did not produce any form of electricity what-so-ever. So, she tried a different approach, but the same thing came out of it. Sure, she got past the making charcoal stage but she could jump the making charcoal electricity hurdle. That was going to be the trickiest part of her whole project. But she was not going to give up. Even if it takes her days, weeks, months and even years to complete this, she'll put everything in her human power to do it. Even if it killed her.

So, she kept trying and trying and trying over and over and over again until one day, she saw a spark. And then another. It was working. It was not electricity, but it was something close to that. That was her 'Eureka' moment. The moment when her months of restless research had come to an end, or at least, looked like it was going somewhere. She had never felt so extremely accomplished. This was everything she has been working for. Even when there was no electricity, she did not pause her research for the slightest bit. There was no way she was giving up now. There was just something she was missing. A little push to get to where she was heading.

Over time, word got to the villagers that Mira was trying to create something in her house. They soon find out it had something to do with the constant smoke coming out her walls and her recurring visits to the village dump. Over time, they got curious to know what she was doing. Some rumours started to spread around the village of Mira being involved in some sort of witchcraft or perhaps a member of some secret society.

Some whose curiosity knew no bounds confronted her about it, to which she gladly told them everything about her way of creating new and resourceful sources of electricity for the whole village and if possible, the country at large. Still, some believed her to be crazy. In fact, most of the people that were curious became uninterested, as they knew her idea would burn to the ground, just like the rest.

But she did not let the words get to her head. She still did what she believed in doing, and shut the whole world out when they called her a crazy witch. All except one, a boy who had been watching her from the side lines. He was intrigued by her outlook on the world. The way that she saw this idea of hers as possible even though the whole world denied it. It was very impressive to him.

That is why when Mira finally left her room with the brightest expression on her face, he immediately wanted to know what was going on. She ran into the village square, jumping up and down and shouting with her little device in her hand. She was happy to show everyone her new invention and a possible game changer for everyone. Basically, the whole village flocked her, staring at her while whispering who knows what to each other. However, Mira did not let this phase her. If anything, it fuelled her up.

She explained to everyone how she came up with a way to make our own electricity and no longer have to sit in darkness anymore. They watched as she connected her machine to the village's light pole and switched it on. It sparked and for a moment, a split second everyone actually felt like Mira was onto something. But its sparks became more violent and unpredictable, so much so that it shot her device, sending it flying into the crowd and leaving the pole burnt up.

At that moment, she had become public enemy number one. Everyone wanted to get her for what she did. But before they could do anything, the boy who had watched from the sidelines jumped between the angry mob and Mira.

"She has tried to help us by showing us we can create our own electricity, and she did it all on her own. Instead of thanking her, you want to attack her!? Have you people lost your minds?" he called.

"If she can come this far alone, imagine how far she can go with us helping her. I believe that if we all put our heads together, we can make this dream come true. After all, teamwork makes the dream work!"

The boy's words tore the crowd, who fell silent in shame. Instead of appreciating her efforts, they realised, they had belittled her project. If it was not doing what everyone wanted it to do, a bit of help would be better.

From that moment on, the village put all their physical and intellectual strengths together to build an electric powerhouse that worked purely on trash (and good vibes). It took them more than a year for the final project to come together, but once it did, everyone enjoyed the outcomes. Neighbouring villages were so impressed by this that they started adopting the model in their own villages, no longer simply waiting for government-provided electricity.

They could make their own electricity. And not only was it free and creative, but it also found a way to dispose of the trash in the village, hence making it solve two problems they faced. Talk about planting two trees with one seed!

Mira had blazed a path for others to follow, so they would no longer need the provisions of government, they could make their own renewable source of power. And she couldn't have done it alone. With the help of one boy, and then her entire village, she pioneered the use of renewable energy as a source of electricity for her community. From that moment, Mira would be a hero in their eyes.

The Whispering Forest

Mahnoor Jamshaid, Pakistan

Amelia had always been fascinated by the Whispering Forest, a dense woodland that bordered her small village. As a child, she had heard tales of the forest's enchanted nature, where trees seemed to whisper secrets to those who ventured deep enough. One warm summer evening, her curiosity got the better of her, and she decided to explore the forest alone. Armed with a small backpack containing a flashlight, a notebook, and a water bottle, she stepped into the forest, feeling a mixture of excitement and apprehension.

The further Amelia ventured, the thicker the canopy above her grew, casting long shadows on the forest floor. The whispers of the trees seemed to grow louder, almost as if they were aware of her presence. She carefully noted down every unusual sight and sound in her notebook. Suddenly, she stumbled upon an old, weathered signpost pointing deeper into the forest. The sign read, "To the Heart of the Forest." Her heart raced with anticipation as she followed the sign's direction.

After walking for what felt like hours, Amelia reached a small clearing bathed in a soft, golden light. In the centre of the clearing stood an ancient oak tree, much larger than any other tree she had seen before. Its trunk was wide and gnarled, and its branches stretched out like welcoming arms. Amelia felt an inexplicable pull towards the tree and instinctively reached out to touch its bark. As her fingers brushed against the rough surface, the whispers around her suddenly grew clearer, forming coherent words.

"Welcome, Amelia," the tree seemed to say. Startled, she stepped back, but the voice continued. "You have been chosen to hear the stories of the Whispering Forest. Long ago, this land was enchanted by a powerful sorcerer who wished to preserve the wisdom and history of the forest. Only those with pure hearts can hear our tales."

As Amelia stood in awe, the ancient oak began to recount its first story. "Many centuries ago, this forest was protected by a guardian named Eldrin. He was a brave and noble elf who dedicated his life to maintaining the balance between nature and the mystical forces that inhabited these woods." The tree's voice was deep and resonant, as if the very essence of the forest was speaking through it.

"Eldrin possessed a magical staff, crafted from the wood of the oldest tree in the forest, which allowed him to communicate with all living creatures. Under his watchful eye, the Whispering Forest thrived, becoming a sanctuary for both the mundane and the magical." Amelia listened intently, her imagination painting vivid pictures of Eldrin and his life in the forest.

"However, darkness soon threatened this harmony. A sorcerer named Malakar, driven by greed and a desire for power, sought to control the forest's magic. He unleashed a blight that began to consume the trees, turning them into lifeless husks. Eldrin knew that the only way to stop Malakar was to confront him directly. In a fierce battle that lasted for days, Eldrin managed to defeat Malakar, but at a great cost."

The oak paused, its leaves rustling softly in the breeze. "Eldrin sacrificed himself to seal Malakar's dark magic. His essence merged with the forest, and his spirit became one with the ancient oak you now stand before. His sacrifice ensured the forest's survival, and his story has been whispered among the trees ever since."

Amelia felt a deep sense of gratitude and sorrow for Eldrin's sacrifice. She realized that the Whispering Forest was not just a place of beauty, but a repository of ancient wisdom and sacrifice. She promised herself to protect the forest and its secrets, just as Eldrin had done.

Inspired by the story of Eldrin, Amelia felt a newfound determination to uncover more of the forest's secrets. She asked the ancient oak if there were other tales it could share. The tree's branches swayed gently as it responded, "There are many stories hidden within this forest. Follow the hidden path behind me, and you will discover another piece of our history."

Amelia carefully made her way around the oak and found a narrow, overgrown trail. As she pushed through the dense foliage, she noticed that the trees seemed to form a natural archway, guiding her deeper into the forest. The whispers grew louder, and she felt as if unseen eyes were watching her progress.

After a short walk, Amelia emerged into another clearing, this one dominated by a crystalline pond. The water was so clear that she could see the bottom, where colourful stones and aquatic plants swayed gently. As she knelt by the edge of the pond, the water began to ripple, and an ethereal figure rose from its depths.

The figure was that of a graceful nymph, her translucent form shimmering in the sunlight. "Greetings, Amelia," the nymph said with a melodious voice. "I am Lira, the guardian of this pond. It holds memories of the forest and its inhabitants. Would you like to hear the tale of the Water Spirit and the Lost Children?"

Amelia nodded eagerly, and Lira began her story. "Many years ago, two children from a nearby village wandered into the forest and became lost. Night fell, and they grew frightened as they struggled to find their way home. Their cries for help reached my ears, and I emerged from the pond to guide them."

"The children were amazed by my appearance, but their fear quickly turned to trust. I led them to this very pond and showed them the way back to their village. In gratitude, they promised to protect the forest and visit me often. Over the years, their descendants have kept that promise, ensuring that the forest remains a safe haven for all."

Amelia was touched by Lira's story and felt a deep connection to the children and their legacy. She realized that her own journey into the forest was part of a larger tapestry of history and magic. She thanked Lira and promised to honour the forest's guardianship, feeling a renewed sense of purpose.

As Amelia continued her exploration, she felt a growing sense of belonging. The forest was revealing its secrets to her, and she felt a responsibility to protect its magic. The whispers of the trees guided her to a secluded glade, where a large, flat stone lay in the centre. On the stone was a glowing amulet, radiating a soft, silvery light.

Amelia carefully picked up the amulet, feeling its warmth in her hands. The ancient oak's voice echoed in her mind, "This is the Moonstone Amulet, a powerful artifact that was created to protect the forest from dark forces. It was crafted by the forest's first guardian, Elara, a wise and powerful sorceress who infused the amulet with her own magic."

"Elara used the amulet to enhance her abilities and maintain the balance between light and darkness in the forest. When she sensed her time was nearing its end, she placed the amulet here, in the heart of the forest, so that a worthy successor could find it and continue her work."

Amelia felt a surge of energy as she put on the amulet. The whispers of the trees became clearer, and she could feel the presence of the forest's magic coursing through her. She knew that she had been chosen to be the forest's new guardian, to protect its secrets and ensure its survival.

With the Moonstone Amulet around her neck, Amelia felt a sense of purpose and destiny. She vowed to uphold the legacy of Elara and Eldrin, to use her newfound abilities to protect the Whispering Forest from any threat that might arise.

As the sun began to set, casting a golden glow over the Whispering Forest, Amelia felt a profound connection to the land and its history. She knew that her life had changed forever, that she was now a part of the forest's legacy. The whispers of the trees filled her mind with wisdom and guidance, and she felt ready to embrace her role as the new guardian.

She returned to the ancient oak, where she had first heard the stories of the forest. The tree's voice was filled with pride and warmth as it spoke. "You have proven yourself worthy, Amelia. The Whispering Forest has chosen you to be its protector. Use the Moonstone Amulet wisely, and remember the stories that have been entrusted to you."

Amelia nodded, feeling a deep sense of honour and responsibility. She promised to protect the forest and its secrets, to ensure that the magic and wisdom of the Whispering Forest would endure for generations to come. As she made her way back to the village, she knew that her life's path had been forever altered.

The villagers welcomed her return with relief and curiosity, sensing the change in her. Amelia shared her experiences with them, ensuring that the stories and lessons of the Whispering Forest would be remembered and respected. She encouraged them to visit the forest, to listen to its whispers, and to honour the legacy of its guardians.

Years passed, and Amelia's connection to the Whispering Forest only deepened. She continued to explore its depths, uncovering new stories and protecting its magic. The villagers, inspired by her dedication, became stewards of the forest as well, ensuring its protection and preservation.

And so, the legacy of the Whispering Forest continued, its stories and secrets safeguarded by those who loved and respected its enchanted beauty. Amelia's journey had only just begun, but she knew that with the guidance of the forest's whispers, she would fulfil her promise as its guardian.

The Vasundhara Storm

Rayshal Tharun HarshaL,
United Arab Emirates

The air in Vasundhara hung thick with tension, a stark contrast to the lush greenery that had once been the city's pride. Avni Sharma, now seventeen, stood at the edge of the polluted river, her fists clenched as she watched another dead fish float by. Three years had passed since Mr. Desai's factory had risen from the ground, a monolithic testament to broken promises and environmental devastation.

She remembered the day the construction began as if it were yesterday. The protests, the impassioned speeches, the hope that had burned so brightly in their young hearts -- all of it had been for naught. Mr. Desai had played his cards well, bribing officials and manipulating the media until the voice of the people was nothing more than a whisper in the wind.

Avni's phone buzzed. A message from Vihaan: "Meeting at the old Neem tree. Now."

At the Neem tree, she found her friends waiting. Vihaan, the tech prodigy, his eyes bloodshot from endless nights of coding. Diya, the artist, her hands stained with paint that could no longer capture the beauty of their dying home. And Varun, the birdwatcher, his binoculars hanging uselessly around his neck -- there were no birds left to watch.

"We've got a problem," Vihaan said, his voice low. "I've been monitoring the factory's emissions. They're not just polluting the river -- they're hiding something much worse."

He pulled out his tablet, showing them a complex graph. "These spikes? They are not normal chemical waste. I think they're dumping some kind of experimental compound."

Avni felt a chill run down her spine. "We need proof. Hard evidence that even Mr. Desai can't deny."

"That's why I called you here," Vihaan said. "I've created a plan to infiltrate the factory. But it is dangerous. If we are caught..."

He did not need to finish the sentence. They all knew the stakes. Mr. Desai's influence reached far beyond Vasundhara. People who opposed him had a habit of disappearing.

Avni looked at each of her friends, seeing the same mix of fear and determination in their eyes that she felt in her heart. "We're in this together," she said. "For Vasundhara. For our future."

As they huddled closer, planning their next move, none of them noticed the drone hovering silently above the Neem tree, its camera focused on their clandestine meeting.

The plan was set. Under the cover of night, Avni and her friends would infiltrate the factory. Vihaan had hacked into the security system, creating a brief window where the cameras would be on a loop. Diya had crafted disguises that would help them blend in with the night shift workers. Varun's keen eye for detail would guide them through the labyrinth of the facility.

At precisely midnight, they made their move. Slipping through a hole in the fence, they darted from shadow to shadow, hearts pounding. The acrid smell of chemicals burned their nostrils, growing stronger as they approached the main building.

Inside, the factory was a maze of pipes and machinery, hissing and clanking in the gloom. They found the control room easily -- too easily, Avni thought. As Vihaan began downloading data from the main computer, Diya kept watch at the door. Suddenly, she hissed, "Someone's coming!"

They scrambled for hiding spots as footsteps approached. From behind a large server, Avni watched as two men entered the room. Her blood ran cold as she recognized one of them: Mr. Desai himself.

"The latest batch is ready," the other man was saying. "But sir, the side effects..."

Mr. Desai cut him off. "I don't care about side effects. This compound will revolutionize agriculture. Imagine crops that grow five times faster, resistant to any pest or disease."

"But the mutations in local wildlife, the effects on the river..."

"Necessary sacrifices," Mr. Desai snapped. "The world will thank us when we solve global hunger. Now, increase production. I want to start human trials next month."

As the men left, Avni's mind reeled. Human trials? This was worse than they had imagined. She looked at her friends, seeing her own horror reflected in their eyes.

But as they crept towards the exit, alarms suddenly blared to life. Red lights flashed, and steel shutters slammed down over doors and windows.

"It's a trap!" Diya cried.

They ran, no longer caring about stealth. But at every turn, they found their path blocked. Cornered in a storage room, they could hear guards shouting, getting closer. Avni's eyes fell on a row of barrels marked with hazard symbols. A desperate plan formed in her mind.

"Vihaan, can you trigger the fire suppression system?"

He nodded, fingers flying over his tablet. Seconds later, sprinklers burst to life, drenching everything in foam.

"Now run!" Avni yelled, pushing over the barrels. A noxious cloud billowed out, mixing with the foam to create a choking fog.

In the chaos that followed, they somehow found their way out, lungs burning, eyes streaming. They did not stop running until they reached the old Neem tree, collapsing in its protective shadow.

Avni's phone buzzed. An unknown number. The message chilled her to the bone: "Did you really think you could challenge me? The game has changed, children. Run while you can."

The following days passed in a blur of fear and frantic activity. Avni and her friends knew they were marked now, their faces plastered across local news channels as "eco-terrorists" who had attacked the factory. Mr. Desai's influence ran deep, twisting their actions into a narrative of mindless vandalism.

They found refuge in an abandoned warehouse on the outskirts of town, converted into a makeshift headquarters by Vihaan's technical wizardry. Surrounded by humming servers and flickering screens, they worked tirelessly to decode the data they had stolen.

But it was not simple. Every time Vihaan tried to upload their findings, the files were immediately taken down. Social media accounts were blocked, emails intercepted. It was as if an invisible wall had been erected around Vasundhara, keeping the truth trapped inside.

One night, unable to sleep, Avni slipped out of the warehouse. She found herself drawn to the river, its waters now a sickly, phosphorescent green in the moonlight. As she stood on the bank, a voice behind her made her jump.

"I thought I might find you here."

Avni whirled to find her grandmother, Anjali, emerging from the shadows. As they embraced, Anjali revealed a long-held secret: "Why do you think Mr. Desai hates our family so much? Your grandfather and I led the protests against his father's logging company thirty years ago. We saved the forest then, but at a great cost."

As Anjali spoke, pieces began to fall into place in Avni's mind. The long-standing feud between their families, the personal vendetta that drove Mr. Desai's actions -- it all made sense now.

"But how do we stop him?" Avni asked, desperation creeping into her voice. "He controls everything."

Anjali's eyes hardened with determination. "Not everything. There are still those who remember the old ways, who understand the true value of our land. We need to remind the people of Vasundhara who they are, where they come from."

A plan began to form in Avni's mind. "A gathering," she said slowly. "Not just a protest, but a celebration of Vasundhara's culture, its connection to the land."

As if on cue, the sound of sirens split the night air. Flashlight beams swept the riverbank as shouts echoed in the distance.

"Go!" Anjali urged, pushing Avni towards the cover of trees. "I'll distract them. Remember, Avni -- the spirit of Vasundhara lives in all of us. Wake it up!"

The next week was a whirlwind of clandestine activity. Avni and her friends worked tirelessly, reaching out to every contact they had in Vasundhara. They spread the word through whispers in marketplaces, coded messages in local radio shows, and ancient symbols painted on walls -- a language of rebellion as old as the hills themselves.

Their plan was audacious: a massive gathering at the heart of the old forest, a celebration of Vasundhara's culture and its deep connection to the land. It would be a statement impossible to ignore, a reminder to the people of what they stood to lose.

But as the day approached, the pressure mounted. Strange accidents befell those who openly supported them. Tension frayed nerves within the group.

One evening, as they argued about the risks, Vihaan suddenly straightened, eyes wide. "Guys, we've got a problem. A big one."

They crowded around his screen. What they saw chilled them to the bone. Amid the lines of code and security protocols was a detailed plan for the next day -- a massive shipment of the experimental compound, set to be released into Vasundhara's water supply during their gathering.

"He's using our event as cover," Avni breathed, horror dawning. "While everyone's distracted..."

"He poisons the entire city," Diya finished.

The magnitude of what they faced crashed over them. This was no longer about saving the forest or exposing corruption. The lives of everyone in Vasundhara hung in the balance.

Avni felt the eyes of her friends on her, waiting for direction. In that moment, she understood the true weight of leadership -- the power to inspire, and the responsibility that came with it.

"Listen to me," she said, her voice steady despite the fear churning in her gut. "Tomorrow isn't just about us anymore. It is about every man, woman, and child in Vasundhara. We might be the only ones who can stop this."

She looked at each of them in turn, assigning crucial tasks. "And I'm going to confront Mr. Desai," she finished.

Protests erupted, but she held up a hand. "We need a distraction. If I can keep him focused on me, it might buy you the time you need."

As dawn broke, they shared a moment of silence, each lost in their own thoughts. Avni looked at her friends -- no, her family -- and felt a surge of love and pride. Whatever happened, they would face it together.

The day of the gathering dawned bright and clear, as if nature itself was holding its breath. Across Vasundhara, people stirred, drawn by an energy they could not quite name. Despite the government warnings to stay home, despite the threats and the fear, they came.

They came in ones and twos at first, then in groups, streaming towards the old forest. Farmers and shopkeepers, teachers, and students, the young and the old -- all converging on the ancient grove that had been Vasundhara's heart for generations.

Avni watched from the edge of the clearing, her heart swelling with emotion. Diya's artwork was everywhere -- vibrant murals and installations that told the story of their land, its beauty, and its peril. Varun led groups through secret paths, whispering the names of plants and animals long forgotten.

But even as hope bloomed, danger loomed. Avni's phone buzzed with updates from Vihaan. The shipment was on the move, heavily guarded. He was doing everything he could to slow it down, but time was running out.

Taking a deep breath, Avni steeled herself for what came next. She kissed her grandmother's cheek, hugged her friends, and slipped away from the gathering. Her destination: the factory.

As she approached the looming structure, alarms blared. Guards poured out, surrounding her. And then, parting the sea of uniforms, came Mr. Desai himself.

"Ah, the prodigal daughter returns," he sneered. "Come to surrender?"

Avni stood tall, channelling every ounce of courage she possessed. "I've come to talk. Just you and me, Mr. Desai. For the sake of Vasundhara."

In his plush top-floor office, Avni confronted Mr. Desai about the true cost of his actions. As they argued, doubt flickered in Mr. Desai's eyes. Then his phone buzzed. As he glanced at it, his expression hardened. "Enough games. Your little friends will not stop my shipment. It's over."

But Avni smiled, a fierce, triumphant smile. "Is it? Look outside."

Frowning, Mr. Desai moved to the window. His jaw dropped. The streets below were filled with people, thousands of them, streaming towards the factory. At their head was Anjali, her voice rising above the crowd: "Remember who you are! Remember Vasundhara!"

At that moment, Avni's phone chimed. A message from Vihaan: "Shipment neutralized. Chemical compounds rendered inert. We did it!"

Mr. Desai's empire was crumbling before his eyes. As the crowd surrounded the factory, as workers laid down their tools and joined the protesters, he sank into his chair, defeated.

"What happens now?" he asked, suddenly looking old and tired.

Avni's voice was firm but kind. "Now, we heal. Together. Vasundhara has always been about balance, Mr. Desai. It's time we remembered that." In the days that followed, change swept through Vasundhara like a cleansing storm. The factory was repurposed, its technology turned towards sustainable energy and truly eco-friendly innovations. Mr. Desai, facing the consequences of his actions, dedicated his considerable resources to undoing the damage he had caused. Avni and her friends found themselves at the heart of a movement that spread beyond their city, inspiring communities across the country to reclaim their environmental heritage.

One evening, as they sat beneath the old Neem tree, tired but content, Diya asked the question they had all been thinking: "What now?"

Avni looked out over their changed home, at the river running clear again, at the new saplings pushing up through the soil. "Now," she said, "we keep going. This was just the beginning." As if in answer, a flock of birds swooped overhead -- species returning to their ancestral grounds. Varun laughed in delight, pointing them out. They laughed, the sound mingling with the rustle of leaves and the distant hum of a city coming back into harmony with its surroundings. Avni closed her eyes, feeling the pulse of Vasundhara strong and steady. They had faced their trial by fire and emerged stronger, wiser. The path ahead was long, but they would walk it together, guardians of a legacy as old as the earth itself. In the heart of Vasundhara, hope bloomed like the first green shoot after a long winter. And the story of four young heroes who dared to change their world was just beginning.

The Moonlight Penguin

Rosie James, New Zealand

Once upon a time in a little brick house on the coast of New Zealand, there lived a small girl called Marina. The beach was her most favourite place because she could peer into busy rock pools full of life and swim with the shining fish, she would dive down to see the waving kelp and patches of white sand. She sometimes used to see groups of Little blue penguins weaving up and down and splashing through the surface of the water, hunting for a fishy meal, but she hadn't seen one in a very long time. Marina loved these birds because they are the world's smallest penguins and they are so agile and clever in their ocean home.

She and her Grandad used their small tin dinghy to bounce over the wild waves and explore the neighbouring bays. They would catch a fish for their dinner often but that was before they started to disappear. Her Grandad said this was because people were taking more fish than they needed on big barges and boats, so Marina stopped having fish for dinner. Every day she walked the sandy shores and every day she noticed the rubbish that washed up, more and more. She found glass bottles, food wrappers, fishing nets, bottle caps, plastic bags, cans, straws, shoes and a plastic chair!

As she was walking and thinking about how the beach never used to have this much rubbish, something caught her eye. A lifeless Little Blue Penguin, its eyes glassy and its small wings twisted in an unforgiving net. It was the first penguin she had seen in months. A shiver ran down her spine, it wasn't fair, poor Penguin, she had to do something, she knew she had to get rid of the rubbish that now ruled the oceans. Why did no one care? She felt angry and kicked a plastic bottle that went flying through the air and bounced off the rocks. Marina could pick up the rubbish, but she couldn't make it go away. What if she used it to turn it into something useful and beautiful?

She could not do it alone and needed to find a solution that everyone could help with. Something practical that could help fix the desperate situation that was developing on her beach. An idea formed in her mind. She ran back excitedly to her little brick house to tell her Grandad about the plan. Marina wanted to hold a meeting in the town hall to tell the people about what was happening to their ocean and ask for help to save the beaches. She spent many days preparing what she would say and researching about the materials that were being washed up on her beach. She practised her speech over and over again until it was etched into her memory. Marina felt so scared to speak in front of the entire town, it would be just awful, but she knew it was what she had to do if she wanted a change.

On the day of Marina's big speech, she combed her hair, practised her talk one more time and nervously rode into the town on her old bike. She stepped into the big hall of beady eyed people, who were all waiting to hear what she had to say. The mayor, who was wearing a striped black tie and a sour expression, boomed at the whispering crowd "to be silent AT ONCE!" Marina took a deep, shaky breath and began to tell her town about the problem with the sea. She told them that their plastic waste was causing marine life to suffer, it was polluting all the beaches and that everyone needed to work together to SAVE OUR OCEANS! She told them about the dead penguin, tangled in the net. As she spoke, Marina could feel herself growing confident and she continued. "We need to stop creating then throwing away more and more plastic and taking more fish than we need, everyone, I need you to help stop this! Please come down to the beach tomorrow and help me pick up the rubbish, then we can recycle the plastic and make something amazing!"

As she finished, she heard evil laughing, the mayor was laughing at her. "You think we will stop pulling fish out of the sea and spend hours picking up trash?!?" He chuckled with a mocking grin, "If Polly Penguin doesn't like plastic, then too bad!"

Marina felt embarrassment bubble up inside her, she had expected the people to agree to help her and cheer. She felt hot tears well in her eyes as she rushed out of the hall in shame. When the next day came, Marina got up early. She was determined to clean the beach even if the community refused to take part. A small pile of plastic bags and bottle tops had started to pile up on the bank when she heard a noise, a faint cheering.

She strained her ears, "Let's save our Sea!" is what she heard over and over, louder and louder. Until she saw it, someone was walking over the hill towards her, followed by another and another, then a huge crowd of people came down the hill to help her. Marina laughed and shouted with delight. She was so happy. She asked the people what had changed their minds. "We didn't change our minds" they said, "We disagreed with the mayor from the start, we just didn't get the chance to tell you before you ran out!"

So, Marina and the people of the town set to work, picking the bottle caps out of the rock pools and pulling the plastic out of the seaweed and sand. After an entire day of rubbish collecting, there was a huge pile on the shore bank. They all looked at their beautiful and now clean beach and admired what a great environment it was without all the plastic mess. Then they started to work on their plan, to make a recycled seaside village.

Marina remembered seeing a video during her research about how someone had made strong and durable fence posts out of recycled plastic, she remembered how they ground up the plastic into pieces and melted them to make a shape, so that's what she did. All the plastic rubbish was cut up into very little pieces and melted over the fire in a tin barrel they had found on the beach. The mixture was stirred around until it was smooth gooey, then it was shaped into cuboid bricks with the wooden moulds they had made. They stacked the bricks on the bank and left them to set. The old planks and boards were used as the sturdy skeletons for the houses which were banged together from the nails from grandad's shed. Tin soda cans could be cut and bent to make a lovely and shiny silver roof.

The plastic bricks made great walls, they used the stained glass from the bottles as windows and the sun shone through, making colours dance across the floorboards. The colourful houses were nestled in the clay banks that line the sea, half way between the beach and the land. Marina and the people of the village decided to add the finishing touches by planting New Zealand's coastal trees, Pohutukawa, all around the plastic houses. Its roots would help with stabilising the earth around the houses and attract native birds. The branches stretched up across the blue sky, there was a tree for every house! Marina used the many bottle caps to make a huge Blue Penguin picture on one of the walls of her house, she looked up at its ocean blue feathers and webbed pink feet, Marina hoped that she had saved at least one Blue Penguins life. She was so proud of the beautiful recycled houses.

The next day she and her Grandad wrote a letter to Marina's lonely great aunt who lived in the far away city and invited her to come and live in one of the seaside houses with colourful windows. And soon Marina's great aunt was joined by many people who wanted to live in the amazing seaside village made by people who were saving the ocean.

No one ever took more fish than they needed and nets were forbidden to enter the sea.

So, a lively community was born and they all joined Marina and her pledge to protect and respect the coasts of New Zealand.

One clear night, a few months later, as Marina was getting ready to go to bed in her little brick house, she heard a strange noise. It sounded like a loud high pitched door creaking and squealing, as she looked out the window to search for the source of the noise, something caught her eye. It was a small shape, silhouetted against the full moon's reflection on the still water.

Then she realised what she had heard was a little blue penguin's call! As she watched, it waddled down across the untouched sand to the water's edge and Marina saw the surface ripple with shining water. It must have been going out to get its breakfast, maybe even to feed a chick! Marina smiled.

The Enduring Girls

Bezawit Ayelign Fentahun, Ethiopia

The month was October. Meron and her friend walked across the expansive field, surrounded by blossoming flowers and various shades of green grasses, which filled them with a sense of contentment. Occasionally, they paused briefly to inhale the unique fragrances of the flowers. They appreciated nature's gift and wished for a long life to continue enjoying it.

Suddenly, Meron said, "It's no use; nature's gifts are often disrupted by people." She exclaimed, "Human beings place an unbalanced burden on nature. How wonderful nature is! Humankind cannot survive without its support."

"Have you heard the elders often talk about the dominance of warm temperatures, recurrent droughts, and the subsequent loss of crops?" Meron's friend said she had heard it often but had not paid much attention. She understood that humans are both enemies and allies of nature. Humans engage in deforestation and reforestation, but the efforts to replace deforested areas usually fall short of expectations.

Meron affirmed that nature does not retaliate against human beings; instead, it is patient. Her friend agreed with Meron's idea but added that nature does have an impact on human beings. She argued that if humans do not manage nature properly, it can lead to significant consequences, such as climate change.

While they were conducting a heated discussion, they heard a scream from a nearby rural village but could not identify which hamlet it came from. This immediately captured their attention. The villagers ran to a hut located at the corner of the village. The village's inhabitants stood sadly in a circle around the hut, simultaneously raising their hands to the sky, seeking God's support for a safe childbirth.

They observed the scene with keen interest. The traditional birth attendant was massaging the pregnant woman's abdomen using traditional butter as a lotion. She seemed to be using forceful rubbing to assist with the difficult labour. Despite these efforts, the woman continued to scream in pain. Surprisingly, the traditional birth attendant shouted at her and warned her to stop screaming.

Melat and her friend were moved to tears by the sight of women in labour. Saddened by the situation, they reflected that it could have been easier if the villagers had access to modern health facilities nearby or if an ambulance were available to transport the women in labour safely.

They were saddened when they heard from the villagers that many women had died while seeking medical help due to unsafe transportation methods, such as being carried on makeshift stretchers. After six hours, the birth attendant announced to all the villagers, "Congratulations!" She had given birth to a baby girl. The community villagers surrounding the labour hut shouted joyfully, all saying, "Congratulations!"

Immediately after the traditional birth attendant congratulated the family on the birth of a girl, the villagers began to gossip, expressing their wish that the baby had been a boy. Surprisingly, the women were the main supporters of this sentiment. Melat and her friend exchanged shocked glances. Suddenly, with an angry tone, Melat exclaimed, "You are not quite right! I'm afraid I have to disagree with your preference for a boy. Who created this misconception? Give me an answer!" All the attendants awkwardly fell silent for a moment. Some whispered that they thought she was losing her mind.

With the silence hanging in the air, Melat groaned, "Gender inequality starts at birth. How foolish is this tradition? How can generations continue if female children are not born? She was challenging a deeply ingrained cultural bias favouring boys over girls. She could not believe her ears when the children in the village loudly chanted, "We like boy children, boy children..."
She laughed in astonishment and sighed in despair. Some stories she heard from her friend astonished her.

She listened attentively as her friend recounted, "I heard from my relatives in remote areas that there is a tradition where a woman is placed in isolation in the forest when it's time to give birth. There, the pregnant woman is forced to give birth alone without any support. They believe she is not purified during that time. Melat's friend realized that the situation in this village was much better than the story she had heard, so she tried to pacify Melat.

Melat was jolted from her deep thoughts when the village priest loudly proclaimed, "The Bible teaches us that females and males are not equal in many things." It seemed like a response to Melat's question. Melat realized that religion also has an impact on gender bias right from birth.

Melat and her friend departed from the village, suspecting that unforeseen dialogue might intensify. Though Melat and her friend departed, there was a discussion among the villagers about Melat and her friend's stance, which did not align with local traditions. Some villagers remarked, "They are like us; who influenced their thinking and speech?" There was no quick and exact answer. Some suspected that Melat had an elder brother who attended university, and he might have taught them.

While crossing to their home, Melat and her friend observed many children engaged in hazardous and laborious activities that critically affected their physical development. They saw children with emaciated and weakened faces. Melat recalled what his elder brother told her about the violation of child rights particularly related to child labour, early marriage, and other child rights in Ethiopia. Ethiopia has indeed taken significant steps to protect children's rights by signing and ratifying international conventions like the Convention on the Rights of the Child (CRC).

Melat's elder brother pursues human rights law. He has studied the protection of child rights in different localities of Ethiopia. He produced several case stories and key findings that can be useful for policy implications. Once upon a time, he was invited to present his research paper abroad with the support of his research advisor. The workshop participants were amazed by the case stories presented by Melat's elder brother. Among the major findings that shocked the major participants were the effects of early marriage on girls' health particularly the prevalence of obstetric fistula. Consequently, they were very often stigmatized and even not allowed to go outside the home. This was witnessed in some pictures like skin discoloration due to lack of sunlight.

He also described the rampant child labour in Ethiopia and its effect on child health, child education, and overall well-being. Due to the high magnitude of child labour, many children were out of school. Following his presentation, several questions were forwarded to him. The participants were deeply interested to know the causes of early marriage and child labour. His response was very short, he said it is poverty. But, most of the participants raised their hands to further elaborate his response. He replied, "In my country mainly in rural communities, having children is considered as economic and social security. This means that the girls' parents get property in the form of bride price while the male child has to earn an income from his labour and is entitled to contribute to his family's income."

Melat's elder brother's research findings resounded well with many of the workshop participants. Their keen interest has resulted in an exchange of their contact addresses with him. While the elder brother stays aboard, Melat and her friend's parents have also arranged marriage for Melat and her friend during their vacation from ninth grade at the age of fourteen. Their parents preferred this time mainly the absence of Melat's elder brother, who had been a strong advocate against early marriage, which likely made it easier for their parents to proceed with these arrangements.

Melat's elder brother has received multiple emails from the workshop participants. Some have also requested partnerships to be part of the solutions. Some others also pledged funding if there is any organization involved in this activity. He thanked all for these positive responses.

For the preparation of the start-up project, he came to his research areas. He knew Melat and her friend disappeared from their parent's home two weeks ago. No one has provided information about Melat and her friend's whereabouts or the reasons for their absence.

In a very distressing situation, one evening a youth brought him a rolled piece of paper. He was in a hurry to read a letter. He opened it quickly and read: "Dear elder brother, please save us; our parents arranged early and forced marriage. We need your prompt support." Melat's elder brother prepared the project implementation and sent it to the donors. They released it for implementation. For this job, he had to employ vibrant children. Melat and her friend were some of the best candidates, particularly for community awareness and child rights advocacy campaigns. He empowered them for this task. The government organizations collaborated with him for success.

Melat and her friend endured a harrowing week hiding in a cave, surviving on wild fruits and drinking water from streams and rivers flowing through the forest. Melat and her friend were deeply grateful for the collaborative efforts of Melat's elder brother and some active community members in their search and rescue. Their parents were given a thorough awareness session about the consequences of early and forced marriages. They realized the severity of their actions and sincerely apologized for their mistakes.

The projects implemented were highly impactful, and Melat, along with her friends, showed a keen interest and worked diligently towards achieving a future free from early marriage and child labour, with access to education for all. At their annual project implementation ceremony, everyone pledged to work diligently towards achieving the key Sustainable Development Goals (SDGs) by 2030 with the full implementation of the Convention on Child Rights. This author wished to see this success and to be part of the solution!

The Orion Problem

Jona David, United Kingdom / Canada / Switzerland / Germany

The night was rapidly aging.

Time seemed to hold its breath, and the world outside was a dark abyss, untouched by any light save the dim glow of his desk lamp.

The Examiner's fingers trembled as he lifted the small grey mug to his lips. The bitter aroma of coffee, its sharp scent like the edge of a razor, twisted into the cold air, mingling with the mustiness of old papers strewn across the desk. The mug was worn, chipped in places, but it was the only thing that offered him a sliver of comfort as he neared the final hours before his deadline.

Writing exams—he mused, wiping a bead of sweat from his brow—was more difficult than many realised. The act was not just about framing questions, crafting traps, or making sure the answers fit within a tightly constructed framework. No, it was about creating a challenge, a moment of testing that could launch minds into new realms of thought, unraveling the very fabric of knowledge. It was about selecting ideas that would persist, that could one day be discussed in university halls, argued over in classrooms, debated long into the night.

He took another sip, the coffee scorching his tongue, trying to shake the unease that clung to him like an ill-fitting coat. He had promised himself he would finish earlier, but each year, the task always seemed to expand, twisting itself into a labyrinth of impossible expectations. They had asked for just one more problem. One more idea. How could he resist? How could he not? Now, though, with the clock ticking away relentlessly, the weight of the unsubmitted work was unbearable.

Only one problem remained to be resolved.

Sequences of numbers spiraled like nebulae through his mind—fractals that interlocked with one another, patterns emerging, slipping away, shifting and reforming. It had been eons since numbers had danced this way, since equations had come alive in such vivid patterns, as if they were trying to tell him something he had forgotten. The problem was there, floating just out of reach. He could feel its structure, its complexity; but the final pieces refused to align. There was a gap. A void.

A memory flashed, as if conjured by the very numbers swirling in his mind.

It was another late evening, years ago, just before their GCSE Free-Standing Maths Qualification examinations. The Examiner's thoughts, now wrapped in age and regret, returned to that time—a time when he was not alone in his intellectual pursuits. Back then, there was Alex, and Orion. They had met during the scholarship selections for secondary school, their meeting a strange collision of fate. The kind of brilliance that sparks instantly between people who speak the same language, who share the same hunger for knowledge.

Alex had been something else entirely—a force of nature. Where the Examiner had relied on precision, on methodical thinking, Alex had an intuitive grasp of mathematics that was almost mystical. He was the kind of person who could solve problems before they were fully formed, whose mind saw the structure of an equation before the ink even touched the page. The Examiner remembered how, over the weeks, a constellation of bright stars had formed between them. Their group—Orion—was an odd formation of personalities, each orbiting around the shared thrill of discovery.

The library cellar became their domain. The room was small and crowded with old books and the smell of stale coffee, but for them, it was a universe unto itself. It was there that their minds, like the stars in the shining constellation whose name they had adopted for their group, came together in a delicate balance. With each challenge, each problem, they found new ways of thinking, new ways of questioning. The problems they tackled became battles of willpower and wit, no conundrum too complex, no traps too treacherous, no equation too elusive. Two once-in-a-generation minds - the neutron star and the black hole - locked in an intricate orbit that drew in others as shining singularities. They were bound together by a magnetic force beyond gravity—a friendship forged in the pursuit of something greater than grades, something purer. An intellectual companionship.

And yet, there was always one who outshone the others. Alex.

Most evenings, they would be practicing. Finding the toughest problems for each other from the numerous past papers on record was their race, their constant challenge. One night, in the dim glow of the library's solitary desk lamp, Alex had pulled out a particularly challenging problem from a forgotten past paper. It was a curveball— patterns and relations all twisted together in a web that seemed as detailed as a galactic cluster. The Examiner and the others had worked tirelessly, pulling at the edges of the problem, trying to find the key. Hours passed as the clock ticked unnoticed, their minds absorbed in the work, consumed by the joy of solving.

But they had failed, all of them. The Examiner could still remember the moment, the one that left him stunned. Alex had looked at them all, unruffled, as though the answer had already come to him. "The proof," he'd said, his voice almost casual, "is only two lines long." The words had hung in the air, taunting them. Alex's mind had always been ahead, faster, sharper. It was as if the rest of them were racing just to keep up with him, to reach a place they knew they could never truly attain. That night, that failure, still haunted him.

The Examiner's thoughts snapped back to the present, as his fingers hovered above the keyboard. The mug in his hand had gone cold now, its contents long emptied, but the sense of urgency still burned within him. The words still echoed in the Examiner's mind, like a refrain. A promise. Or a challenge.

He typed in Alex's last problem, the one he had never fully explained, the one that continued to elude their group after that final night. The one Alex had whispered about as a parting message, perhaps with a knowing smile.

With a resigned sigh, he clicked the 'send' button, pushing the problem into the digital ether, where it would either find its place in the world or fade into the noise of forgotten calculations. He stared at the screen for a long time, the flickering of the cursor a reminder of how much time had passed, of how little had been solved.

Unable to help himself, he reached for the old album labeled "Orion" sitting at the edge of his desk. The album had been with him for years—through triumphs and tragedies, through the passing of time. He turned the pages slowly, each photograph, each scribbled note, a piece of his past.

And then he arrived at the final page, the last snapshot, the one he had always turned away from, wincing.

The photograph was faded now, the edges curling with age, but it still held its weight. Alex's country had been invaded and he had rushed home for conscription, to protect his sisters.

The Examiner remembered the day the photograph had arrived, weeks after Alex's death—a final tribute, a posthumous honour. Alex, smiling awkwardly in ill-fitting fatigues, next to a captured tank. His brilliant mind, able to discern and disarm the most subtle of mathematical traps, had not seen that the armoured vehicle was wired to detonate...

The Examiner's vision blurred as he stared at the image, the grief rushing forward like a wave, threatening to overwhelm him. He blinked rapidly, refocusing on the photograph. It was the injustice that still pierced him, after all these years. There had been no honour, no glory, just a pitiful loss of the one of the brightest stars in the firmament.

Removing the photograph in the half-gloom, he held it to the glowing red ember of his desk lamp. Faint words appeared on the back, a message from long ago, finally visible in the heat. In the corner of the image, faint, almost invisible words had appeared, only visible now after years of gentle handling:

"I lied. The impossible problem wasn't from a past paper - it was mine. And so is the solution. Good luck."

The Examiner laughed helplessly, a hollow sound that echoed through the empty room. He closed the album slowly, his heart heavy with the weight of memories and wasted potential.

Weeks later, the British Maths Olympiad opened its papers to a galaxy of eager students. The neutron stars and supernovae of their generation stared in hopeless dismay at Problem Five. Orion shone before them, an insurmountable challenge.

Saving Cedaria

Sophia Jalkh, Lebanon

Amal had become accustomed to waking up to sirens every other day; sirens that sounded loudly every time a piece of Cedaria exhaled its last breath. Amal was just as breathless as her planet. Her heart throbbed with every warning of nearing doom. And so, she had made it her mission to explore what was left of Cedaria's miracles before they were to fade away indefinitely. Little did she know she would be the one to save her planet.

Amal and her two best friends Laila and Karim carefully crafted a month-long itinerary for their summer, making sure to cover all destinations that were still standing. Meanwhile, havoc had started overriding Cedarians' daily routines. With clean water shortages and disappearing energy resources, schedules were fairly disturbed. Despite such disarray, the citizens felt no urgency towards stimulating change in their way of life. Instead, they blamed it on inherent fate and customary variations of nature.

Calamity had been knocking on Cedaria's door for quite a while now. In fact, warnings of near catastrophes had become a ritual. Despite all this chaos, the people of Cedaria lived in denial. They could see their home slowly crumbling down in front of their eyes, but they could not feel it. Greed, voracity, and insatiability had been nibbling away at their minds and souls for far too long, and they were now desensitized to all and any forms of remorse.

Cedaria had once been a marvel of a planet, adorned with natural gems. Mountains covered with diamonds of pearly white snow feeding into blue glassy rivers that flow amid hills embroidered with countless multicolour shrubs. Lava moulded into cone-like volcanoes that spread out into stretches of golden specs intertwined with sparkling cerulean beaches. Pink and purple cotton candy clouds hanging from the pale blue sky like expensive Christmas ornaments. Rocks and boulders that attest to a God that had taken the time to carefully sculpt each one into the kind of statues museums fight over displaying. Forests of ancient trees painted in every shade of green, with wooden trunks carved into what seemed like warm familiar faces. Cascades of crystal carrying tiny aquafae, sending them off into glazed aquamarine lakes.

Cedaria was one of a kind. But its people had been too selfish for too long, and so the reign of its beauty was coming close to an end. With jungles of concrete, piles of pale green bills, and collections of riches making the top of every inhabitant's priority list, the planet's nature had been completely neglected for decades.

Virtues like life on land, life under water, and sustainable cities, simply did not matter to those who could not see beyond the tip of their noses. The people of Cedaria had become so used to their egocentrism that they had developed a sort of self-destructing tunnel vision.

Nonetheless, Amal would wake up every day and check her calendar, ticking off whichever landmark she and her friends were visiting from her bucket list for the day. She would pace along her withering garden to cross the street and meet with her friends.

Trip after trip, Amal and her friends could clearly see the vividness of the landscapes wilting away. Rivers were drying out with discoloured fish floating atop the still dark water, naked trees bending towards the floor as if to admit defeat, whiny animals awaiting their death amid already dying forests. Oceans so saturated with trash to the point where one could barely tell if piles were moving in water or with the wind. The rising temperatures suffocating the three best friends that were once capable of enjoying the weather on their adventures rather than viewing it as a menace

However, Amal suffered the repercussions of Cedaria's slow death differently than others. She felt it from within. While her friends were falling sick from drinking polluted water, and her parents from breathing in toxins, and while her grandparents' gardens disappeared into the wrath of forest fires, Amal was hurting with Cedaria. It was almost as if Amal and Cedaria shared the same pulse. With time, and especially with the increasing frequency of her adventures into Cedaria's deepest natures, Amal began to notice that she was sharing the planet's pain on a deeper level. She watched as others dealt with standard "scientific" impacts without showing an ounce of grief or penitence and thought to herself: "What's wrong with me?". A concoction of guilt, shame, and sorrow growingly haunted her with every dreary day on her beloved planet.

One day, as she stepped into the great forests of Tanneria, Amal would lay her hand carefully onto the aching trunks of the ancient trees. For a moment, she could have sworn she heard a voice calling to her: "Help us". She then felt her arm go numb and her fingers tingle with pain. On another occasion, she was walking by the Afqian waterfalls when she felt a sharp pain in her knee that spread into the rest of her leg. With such occurrences accumulating, Amal eventually pinned down the fact that they were unique to her, and only her. At first, she believed herself to be cursed and doomed to ache with Cedaria's perishing soul. But with time, she understood that she was in fact gifted.

Amal grew curious of her abilities, which drove her to try connecting with the flora and fauna more often, even when she was not on some grand trip with Karim and Laila. After some time, Amal mastered this power of hers, learning how to communicate with Cedaria by listening to what the primeval realms were telling her. Whispering flowers, humming waves, rustling leaves, rasping stones, and chirping birds. Cedaria was pulling on its every last string to guide Amal into reversing and the people's damage. Luckily, Amal caught onto the signs, and so Karim and Laila shared her efforts in trying to figure out the extent of her gift.

They would sit out every day in Amal's backyard trying to think of ways she could utilize her abilities to fulfil Cedaria's wish. On a gloomy afternoon, the three best friends walked east from town to the Mezin river. As they arrived, Amal could feel Cedaria's distress creeping up her spine. She and Karim were carefully hopping from rock to rock, when she misplaced her foot on a slippery boulder and fell into the stagnant water filled with moribund creatures. Amal felt every nerve in her body shoot up with agony. Her friends stood there, mouth agape, as Amal's wails echoed through the woods. Bewilder took over them as they tried to understand, for Amal could not have been physically hurt, as the shallow river was still and there were no sharp rocks beneath her. Then, within a split second, Karim jumped in after her, grabbing her arms and pulling her onto the riverbank as quickly as he possibly could. As his rough palms grazed Amal's wet forearms, he too felt a searing pain overtaking every fibre of his being. He instantly let go of his grip on Amal and felt his symptoms disappear.

"What just happened?!"Karim screamed. "Did you feel that?"

"Feel what?", said Amal as she struggled to steady her breath. She was not screaming anymore, and her suffering had dissipated. "I felt your pain! When I touched you...", stammered Karim as he tried to make sense of what he was saying. He reached out his hand and flicked his fingertip against Amal's arm again. He felt a mild shock zap throughout his arm and jerked away. "Laila, you try now," Karim ordered, as he pushed her towards Amal. The same thing happened to her as well.

The three best friends retired back home where they scratched every corner of their brains to understand what had occurred. They revisited every detail, every movement, and even tried to recreate the scene in the coming days. Ultimately, they realized Amal's gift was not merely hers. It was one that she could share with others. Not only could she feel Cedaria's misery, but she could allow others to feel it too by touching them. Amal and her friends showed this gift to almost everyone they knew. From their families to their peers, and from their neighbours to their school teachers. They even made sure to tell Tony, the owner of the local market.

Amal filled up with hope as she could see people's faces change when they realized how much anguish they were putting their planet through. Regret and shame clouded their eyes. Amal was finally on the right track. She knew exactly what needed to be done.

The annual Cedaria holiday was coming up, which all the planet's leaders would be attending. From the president to the parliament, and from business owners to corporation executives. In other words, those with the power to damage, and possibly heal, Cedaria. This was in addition to the public masses that were also regulars of the monumental gathering.

Amal, Karim, and Laila decided this would be the best opportunity to make Cedaria's careless people, and especially those in power, understand the severity of their actions and their consequences. Convincing mere citizens would never be enough; it was those sleeping on beds of money that were truly pivotal. And this was the perfect opportunity to get to them.

They plotted carefully and began executing their plan a week in advance. The trio made a list of people needed to guarantee their success. On the day of the colossal event, Amal, Karim, Laila, and all of their friends, family, and townsfolk marched into the crowds with a set goal in mind. They settled into their peripheral positions, creating ripples of semi-circles among the rest of the people.

The event began and so did the endless bore of "Welcome's" and "Thank You's" too. And when the president came up to give his speech, Amal signalled the initiation of her plan to the rest of her partners. She took a deep breath and glanced left at Karim, and right at Laila. The three best friends smiled at each other and chained their hands together. Then, like dominoes, all those involved intertwined their knuckles. Howls of torment erupted, leaving everyone utterly baffled, jaws visibly dropping to the floor in perplex and fear.

Seconds later, they unanimously nudged into the people surrounding them, merely brushing their skin. The cries of the masses sniped in every direction.

No one could understand what was happening and what had taken over all these people. The president yelled on the microphone begging for them to stop their ear-shattering screams. Once his attention was fully on the crowd, Amal yanked her hands from Laila's and Karim's, and leaped in the direction of the stage as fast as she could. The screams had settled down, with confused stares and murmurs usurping control. Amal had made her way up to the main podium. Security guards and other speakers on stage, even the president, were too stunned to react to her grabbing the microphone, her body wholly heaving as she tried to catch her breath.

"People of Cedaria, my name is Amal. As absurd as it may sound, I have the power to feel the pain of our planet. As it grows weaker, so do I. What you all just felt was a result of our indirect contact. So as of now, you too have felt the agony of Cedaria. I urge you to empathize with our home. It is time we put an end to reckless urbanization and rash exploitation. It is time we prioritized our planet's health, as well as ours, over unsustainable fortune."

Amal glanced over her shoulder at the president as her tiny steps closed the gap separating them. She took his hand. He yelled out in hurt and his knees dropped to the ground, his hands rocking his heavy head. And from that day on, Cedaria's sombre skies finally cleared up bit by bit, as reform and amends swept across the planet. Sirens faded away. Cedaria was thriving once again, and so was its people.

Anik's Promise

Naomi Kene, Canada

In the small town of Aklavik, nestled in the Northwest Territories of Canada, the Northern Lights danced across the night sky, casting an ethereal glow over the snow-covered landscape. Twelve-year-old Anik stood outside his family's log cabin, his breath forming little clouds in the crisp air. The lights, known as aurora borealis, had always filled him with wonder and a sense of magic. Anik's people, the Inuvialuit, had lived in harmony with nature for generations, respecting the land that provided them with everything they needed.

However, in recent years, Anik had noticed troubling changes. The winters were warmer, the ice was thinner, and the animals they relied on were becoming scarcer. One evening, Anik's grandfather, Kallik, gathered the family around the fire. His face, lined with wisdom, was grave. "The land is not speaking to us," he said. "Climate change is threatening our way of life. If we do not act, our traditions and the future of our children are at risk." Anik listened intently. He had learned about climate change in school, but hearing his grandfather speak made the issue feel immediate and personal.

He knew that to protect their land and culture, they needed to embrace both tradition and innovation. Inspired by his grandfather's words, Anik decided to take action. He gathered his friends and formed the Aurora Club, named after the Northern Lights that symbolises hope and renewal. Their mission was to raise awareness about climate change and promote sustainable living in their community. Their first project was to reduce the town's reliance on fossil fuels. Anik had read about solar panels and how they could harness the sun's energy, even in the Arctic. With the help of their science teacher, Ms. Roberts, the Aurora Club applied for a grant to install solar panels on the school's roof. The project was a success, and soon other buildings in Aklavik followed suit. The town began to see the benefits of renewable energy, from reduced electricity bills to a decrease in pollution.

Encouraged by their progress, the Aurora Club turned their attention to sustainable fishing practices, ensuring that the local fish population could thrive for generations to come. One day, while exploring the ice fields with his best friend, Kira, Anik stumbled upon a worrying sight. Several seal pups were stranded on thin ice patches, far from their usual hunting grounds. Anik and Kira, without scaring the little ones, gently pushed them back towards their colonies, then hid behind a small hill watching until the pups were gathered by older relatives. The children reported their findings and actions to the Aurora Club. The situation highlighted the urgent need to address not just local but also global environmental issues.

The club decided to expand their efforts. They organised a community meeting, inviting elders, hunters, and local leaders to discuss the changes they had observed. The meeting was a blend of traditional wisdom and modern scientific knowledge. Elders shared stories of past winters and migration patterns, while younger members presented data on climate trends and projections. The discussions led to actionable plans. The community agreed to monitor wildlife more closely, document changes, and share this information with scientists and policymakers. They also decided to implement more sustainable hunting practices and to educate neighbouring communities about the importance of environmental stewardship. As the winter approached, Anik felt a growing sense of accomplishment. The community had come together, blending traditional knowledge with modern technology to create a more sustainable future.

One night, as he stood beneath the shimmering auroras, Anik felt a deep connection to the land and his ancestors. He knew they were on the right path. But the journey was far from over. Anik and the Aurora Club continued their efforts, organising educational workshops, planting trees to combat erosion, and advocating for stronger environmental policies at the regional level. Their work inspired other communities across the Arctic to take similar steps, creating a network of young environmental leaders.

Later, on a spring day, Anik received a letter from the United Nations. It was an invitation to speak at a conference on climate change and sustainable development. Nervous but determined, Anik travelled to New York City, where he shared his community's story with leaders from around the world. His message was clear: to protect our planet, we must listen to the voices of indigenous peoples and support local, sustainable initiatives. The conference was a turning point. Inspired by Anik's speech, nations pledged to increase efforts to combat climate change and support sustainable development, particularly in vulnerable regions like the Arctic.

As the years passed, Anik's work, creating a network of communities committed to sustainability, remained steadfast. Anik, now a young adult, continued to lead with passion and vision. He travelled across Canada and beyond, sharing the story of Aklavik and advocating for policies that prioritised environmental health and indigenous rights. Back in Aklavik, life continued with renewed hope. The ice grew thicker, the fish more abundant, and the Northern Lights shone even brighter, a testament to the resilience and unity of the Inuvialuit people. Anik knew the road ahead would still be challenging, but he also knew that with determination and collaboration, they could build a future where both their culture and the environment could thrive.

One summer, the Aurora Club hosted a gathering of Arctic communities in Aklavik. Representatives came from Greenland, Alaska, and Siberia, each bringing stories of challenges and triumphs. The event was a celebration of resilience and a platform for sharing solutions. Together, they drafted a declaration calling for global action to protect the Arctic and its peoples.

During the gathering, Anik received a visit from a scientist who had been studying the Arctic for decades. Dr Williams was impressed by the community-led initiatives and their impact. He proposed a partnership between the Aurora Club and his research team to further study the effects of climate change and develop adaptive strategies. The collaboration brought new resources and knowledge to Aklavik. The community became a model for integrating scientific research with traditional knowledge. Together, they developed innovative solutions, such as floating gardens to ensure food security and advanced monitoring systems to track environmental changes.

Anik's leadership and the success of the Aurora Club were recognized globally. He was invited to join international panels on climate policy and sustainable development. Despite the accolades, Anik remained grounded, always returning to his roots and the land that had shaped him. One crisp winter night, as Anik stood once more beneath the Northern Lights, he reflected on the journey. The auroras still filled him with wonder, but now they also represented the promise of a future where humanity and nature thrived together. The path had been long and fraught with challenges, but the vision of a sustainable, just world was within reach. With a deep breath, Anik made a silent promise to the land and to the future generations: to continue the fight for a better world, guided by the wisdom of his ancestors and the unity of his people. The Northern Lights flickered in response, a celestial agreement to the enduring commitment of a young leader and his community.

Years passed, and Anik's work remained steadfast. As climate change continued to impact the Arctic, new challenges emerged. Unpredictable weather patterns, melting permafrost, and shifting animal migration routes demanded constant vigilance and adaptation. One significant issue that arose was the impact of thawing permafrost on the town's infrastructure. Buildings and roads began to show signs of damage as the ground beneath them shifted. Anik and the Aurora Club collaborated with engineers and architects to design resilient structures that could withstand the changing conditions. They implemented innovative building techniques, using materials that could adapt to the fluctuating temperatures and shifting ground. Meanwhile, the Aurora Club's educational initiatives expanded.

They created a comprehensive curriculum on climate change and sustainability, incorporating both scientific knowledge and traditional Inuvialuit practices. This curriculum was adopted by schools across the Arctic, empowering the next generation with the tools they needed to continue the fight for their environment. Anik also recognized the importance of cultural preservation. He spearheaded projects to document and revive traditional Inuvialuit knowledge, from language and storytelling to hunting and crafting techniques. These efforts ensured that the cultural heritage of the Inuvialuit people would be preserved and passed down, even as they navigated the challenges of a changing world. One innovative project involved the creation of digital archives.

Anik worked with tech experts to develop a platform where elders could share their knowledge and stories. This platform became a valuable resource for both the Inuvialuit community and researchers worldwide, highlighting the deep connection between indigenous knowledge and environmental stewardship. As part of their ongoing advocacy, the Aurora Club organised annual summits, bringing together leaders, scientists, and activists from around the world. These summits became influential forums for discussing climate policy and sharing best practices. Anik's vision of a united global effort to combat climate change was becoming a reality.

However, not all was smooth sailing. One winter, a severe storm hit Aklavik, causing widespread flooding due to the unusually warm temperatures that melted large sections of ice. Homes were damaged, and vital supplies were lost. The community was in crisis. The Aurora Club sprang into action, coordinating relief efforts. They, in collaboration with the local government, provided emergency shelter, distributed food and medical supplies, and helped repair damaged homes. Anik led the efforts, working tirelessly alongside his friends and neighbours. Despite their resilience, the storm was a stark reminder of the increasing unpredictability and severity of the challenges they faced due to climate change. Realising that they needed a long-term solution to such events, Anik proposed the construction of elevated structures and better flood defences.

With the help of engineers and additional funding from environmental organisations, they began to build these new structures, designed to withstand extreme weather conditions. The project took several months, but eventually, Aklavik was better prepared for future storms. Amidst his tireless work, Anik found moments of personal joy. He married Kira, his childhood friend and fellow environmentalist. Together, they raised their children with the same values of respect for the land and commitment to sustainability. Their home became a model of eco-friendly living, incorporating renewable energy, sustainable materials, and a thriving garden. Anik's family life and his work were deeply intertwined. His children grew up participating in Aurora Club activities, learning from both their parents and the community. They were taught how to fish sustainably, respect wildlife, and understand the importance of their cultural heritage.

One poignant moment came when Anik's grandfather, Kallik, passed away. The community gathered to honour his memory, sharing stories of his wisdom and strength. Anik felt a profound sense of loss, but also a renewed commitment to continue his grandfather's legacy. The Northern Lights were particularly vibrant that night, a reminder of the enduring connection between past, present, and future. During the ceremony, Anik spoke, his voice steady but filled with emotion. "My grandfather taught me to listen to the land and to our people. His wisdom guided us through many challenges, and it is now up to us to carry his teachings forward. We face many threats, but we also have the strength and unity to overcome them. Together, we will continue to protect our land, our culture, and our future."

As he looked up at the Northern Lights, Anik felt a deep sense of peace and determination. He knew that his grandfather's spirit would always be with him, guiding him as he led his community toward a brighter, more sustainable future. The auroras shimmered above, a celestial promise that the Inuvialuit people and their way of life would endure, shining as brightly as the lights in the Arctic sky.

The World Where We Were Not Left Behind

Sarah Bahraki, United Kingdom

If you are not a dreamer, then where does the thinking of change come from? Change is born in the hearts of those who see the world not just as it is, but as it could be—dreaming that we lay the foundations of a brighter tomorrow, where the whispers of our hopes become the reality of our deeds. I am a dreamer, and in my dreams, I find the seeds of change. Are you a dreamer too?

It was a glorious summer day beneath the vibrant expanse of the azure sky. My friends and I, with hearts full of excitement and the spirit of adventure, decided to embark on a journey. The summer holidays had just begun, presenting the perfect opportunity to explore every hidden corner of our beloved country. This land, which had long been veiled in the shadows of insecurity, was now beckoning us with the promise of newfound freedom. Specifically for women, this journey represented more than mere exploration; it was a reclaiming of spaces once deemed inaccessible.

Our journey commenced from the ancient and storied land of Badakhshan, winding its way towards the bustling heart of Kabul. As we began our travels, a sense of astonishment enveloped us. The air, once thick with pollution, was now clean and crisp, caressing our faces as we drove. The necessity of wearing masks had become a relic of the past. The oppressive cultural barriers that had once confined us had crumbled; we could drive freely, unshackled by outdated norms. Women, once restricted, now moved with the same liberty as men.

Our first destination was Baharak, a town that held the promise of the unknown. We ventured forth to the majestic heights of Pamir. After two hours of driving, we reached a juncture where, in days gone by, vehicles would have had to halt. The treacherous roads would force travellers to continue on foot, navigating perilous paths. But now, to our amazement, the roads had been rebuilt, paving the way for an uninterrupted journey. We marvelled at the sweeping vistas of the mountains, their peaks kissing the heavens. Deciding to stay overnight, we parked our car and set out to explore the city.

What greeted us was beyond our wildest imaginings. The city, which had once been bereft of educational infrastructure, now boasted well-constructed schools. This revelation left us in awe, for Pamir had been a place where the concept of schooling seemed a distant dream. Even the nearby areas, once neglected, now flourished with schools and hospitals. The people no longer needed to undertake arduous journeys to access medical care; it was available at their doorstep. The government had made strides in preventing floods from wreaking havoc on homes, ensuring the safety and stability of its citizens.

Our journey continued to Parwan, where further transformations awaited us. The climate had shifted, bringing with it a breath of fresh air and hope. Upon reaching Kabul, we were met with scenes that filled our hearts with joy. Gone were the days when children roamed the streets, begging for morsels of bread. Now, they attended school, their faces alight with the promise of a better future. Poverty, once a relentless scourge, had receded, and no longer did families have to endure the heart-wrenching decision of selling their children to survive. As we travelled through different provinces, a tapestry of change unfolded before our eyes. The people were more educated, their minds illuminated by the light of knowledge. Quality education was no longer a distant dream but a tangible reality in our once underdeveloped nation. Electricity flowed through the veins of our country, bringing with it progress and possibility. The pain that had once etched itself into the eyes of our people, the anguish of losing loved ones to war, had diminished. Fear had given way to hope, and the haunting farewells of families torn apart by violence were a thing of the past. I no longer heard the heart-breaking tales of those forced to flee their homes, leaving behind everything they held dear. I, too, had returned to my homeland, no longer a refugee, no longer an outsider burdened with the weight of displacement. The word 'refugee' had become a forgotten relic, as people no longer fled out of necessity but by choice, seeking new horizons rather than escaping peril. I was a traveller, not a refugee; my home was secure, my neighbours no longer mourned the loss of loved ones to war or natural disasters. The world no longer viewed us through the lens of poverty; we were equals, standing tall in the global community.

Our journey, once a dream, had become a reality. We revelled in the peace and progress that now defined our nation. The roads we travelled were not just physical paths but symbolic of the journey our country had undertaken. Each mile marked a step towards a brighter future, a future where every individual could dream and achieve without fear or limitation.

In Baharak, the sun's golden rays illuminated the landscape, casting a warm glow over the fields. Farmers worked with a sense of purpose, their efforts no longer hampered by outdated tools or techniques. Modern agricultural practices had taken root, ensuring bountiful harvests and food security for all. The villages buzzed with life, their streets bustling with activity. Markets thrived, offering an array of goods and services, a testament to the economic revival that had taken hold.

Pamir, once a region shrouded in mystery and isolation, had become a beacon of education and health. The schools, with their sturdy walls and vibrant classrooms, were filled with eager students. Children, who once had little hope of receiving an education, now dreamed of futures filled with promise. The hospitals, equipped with advanced medical facilities, provided care and comfort to the sick and injured. The people of Pamir no longer faced the grim choice between seeking medical help and staying close to home.

As we travelled through Parwan, the changes were evident in every aspect of daily life. The government's efforts to mitigate the effects of flooding had borne fruit, protecting homes and livelihoods. The infrastructure improvements had transformed the region, making it resilient in the face of natural disasters. The climate, once harsh and unforgiving, had become more temperate, fostering a sense of well-being among the inhabitants.

Kabul, the heart of our nation, stood as a testament to our collective resilience and determination. The city, once scarred by conflict, had risen from the ashes, embodying the spirit of renewal. Children played in the streets, their laughter a melody of hope. Schools were filled with eager minds, and the sight of children begging for food had become a distant memory. The streets, once lined with makeshift homes, now showcased modern buildings and green spaces. The poverty that had once gripped the city had loosened its hold, replaced by a sense of opportunity and growth.

Our journey took us through the diverse provinces of our country, each one a unique thread in the tapestry of progress. In the rural areas, we witnessed the transformation brought about by education. Adults and children alike embraced learning, recognizing it as the key to a better future. Literacy rates had soared, and vocational training programs equipped individuals with skills to secure gainful employment. The empowerment of women was particularly striking, as they took on leadership roles and contributed to the development of their communities.
In the urban centres, we marvelled at the advancements in technology and infrastructure. The availability of electricity had revolutionized daily life, powering homes, businesses, and industries. Access to clean water and sanitation facilities had improved health outcomes, reducing the prevalence of diseases. The economy had diversified, with thriving sectors such as manufacturing, services, and tourism. The entrepreneurial spirit was alive and well, with start-ups and small businesses driving innovation and job creation.

The most profound change, however, was in the hearts and minds of the people. The pain that had once been etched into their faces had given way to a sense of hope and optimism. The fear of losing loved ones to war had diminished, replaced by a sense of security and peace. The stories of separation and loss, once all too common, had become rare. Families were no longer torn apart by violence or displacement. Communities had become more cohesive, united by a shared vision of a brighter future.

As I travelled through my country, I was filled with a deep sense of pride and gratitude. The journey we had undertaken was not just a physical one, but a journey of transformation and healing. Our nation had overcome immense challenges, emerging stronger and more resilient. We had built a society where every individual had the opportunity to thrive, where dreams could be realized, and where no one was left behind.

In this new world, I no longer felt like a refugee. I was a traveller, exploring the beauty and diversity of my homeland. My heart was at peace, knowing that my country had become a place of safety and opportunity. The word 'refugee' had lost its significance, as people no longer fled out of desperation but chose to explore new horizons out of curiosity and ambition. My home was no longer a place of sorrow and loss, but a sanctuary of hope and possibility.

As I continued my journey, I encountered people from all walks of life, each with their own story of resilience and triumph. I met farmers who had transformed their lands through sustainable practices, educators who had dedicated their lives to nurturing young minds, and entrepreneurs who had built thriving businesses from the ground up. Each person I met was a testament to the power of human spirit and the capacity for change.

In the peaceful villages, I listened to the stories of elders who spoke of the days of struggle and sacrifice. They recounted tales of perseverance and determination, of communities coming together to rebuild their lives. Their wisdom and experience were invaluable, guiding the younger generation as they forged their own paths. The bonds of family and community had been strengthened, creating a sense of belonging and support.

In the bustling cities, I witnessed the vibrancy of modern life. The streets were filled with the sounds of laughter and music, the sights of innovation and creativity. I wish never to open my eyes and see this world vanish, never to wake from this beautiful dream. I want this world to be real, a world where we were never left behind.

The Legacy of the Blue Macaw

Carina Araujo, United States of America

He was happily flying through the Amazon Rainforest here in Brazil. He was just a blue macaw looking for food for my babies. He flew through enormous trees with such fresh green leaves. He travelled through rivers and lakes. He saw many animals that lurk in murky dark places, and he spotted his friend the Toucan. He was trying to find Castanha do Para (Brazil nuts) to feed his chicks. And there he saw it: one of the biggest Brazil nuts he had ever seen. He quickly plucked some from the grand tree and flew to his nest. Even before reaching the nest, he could imagine his chicks wailing and fighting over the nuts. When he was just about to arrive, he began to smell smoke.

A huge grey cloud of carbon was gushing up into the air. There were tones of orange, yellow, red, and even white dancing in the sky as if they were clashing to see which one could reach the highest and do the most damage. Suddenly, he spotted a notorious farmer who was the one responsible for this disastrous event. He saw his employees laughing happily at the sight of the fire. They did not care as long as they were making money. They were even happy about it. These were not good people, but the blue macaw still trusted humanity, and he knew there were good people out there. There was a boy who resembled the notorious farmer. They looked so much alike, with the same brown hair, tan skin, and brown eyes. They could only be father and son. His father must have been trying to show his son his "grand" work. To the blue macaw, his work was not grand, it was destructive. Unfortunately, these fires were occurring more often. Suddenly, a frightening thought came across him: the fire was near his nest. His stomach churned from anxiety. "My chicks!" He recalled. His chicks, as well as many other animals, were going to die. He had to save them. He yelled "caw, caw" but heard no answer. He finally reached his nest, avoiding the dancing colours and the choking smoke. His nest! His chicks! The smoke and dust had killed them. Sadly, his chicks were no more. He remained silent. He could not move.

After a few seconds that seemed like eternity, he saw the notorious farmer and employees leaving but not the son. He grabbed his chicks hoping that the son would not notice them and shoot the blue macaw for his beautiful feathers. He put his chicks on the scorched ground and nudged them, still with hope that they would get up, but they did not. He sobbed about the loss of his once beautiful nest and chicks. That is why you should never name your chicks in the first year of their lives as they may get shot or killed. However, he secretly named them, which made him ache even more. The son was approaching, and the blue macaw was too sad and weak, too exhausted to fly away. Instead of killing the blue macaw, the son wrapped the three chicks in an embroidered cloth and buried them. All animals can speak the language of their own country, but the chicks did not have enough time to learn the language. Animals do not normally talk to humans, but the blue macaw made an exception. "You are not like your father. You do not want to destroy things or hurt anyone. Thank you for not killing me and for gently burying my chicks, which is something I could never have been able to do. Thank you!" said the blue macaw.

The boy's facial expression made it clear that he was in awe. His mouth and eyes were wide open. He was utterly flabbergasted. He was not responding. Of course! He must have just been too shocked. So, the blue macaw began talking again, "Animals normally do not talk to humans, but we can still learn your language. Tell me, what is your name?"

The boy reluctantly said, "Uh, my name is Jorge."

"Now Jorge, stop staring at me as if I spoke a foreign language and listen to me. Stand up to your father and tell him that he is damaging the environment, destroying my home and killing innocent animals."

"I cannot say that to my father. First, I do not have the courage to do so. Second, how can I tell my father that he is causing much damage if he is producing food for all of us to eat?" said Jorge.

The blue macaw retorted, "Animals and trees in the rainforest are not the only ones affected by the destruction of the rainforest. Everyone is. The Amazon Rainforest produces twenty percent of our oxygen, takes in carbon dioxide, and is home to one third of all animals and plant species in the world. Cutting down trees releases carbon dioxide, which get trapped, causing temperatures to rise and causing more frequent and extreme weather events like droughts, wildfires, and tornados. Indigenous people live in the rainforest too. They would lose thousands of their stories and beliefs if we lost the Amazon rainforest. Animals and trees would be the ones to suffer first from your actions, but later humans will learn that they will suffer even more. Now, do you understand why you should help?"

Jorge shot back, "Surely there is too much of the Amazon rainforest left for anything like that to happen, right?"

The blue macaw replied disappointingly "You are so wrong! Unbelievably, almost twenty percent of the forest is gone and over two hundred thousand acres are burned every day."

"How terrible! Alright then, I will help!" Jorge asserted.

"Are you going to tell your father, Jorge?"

Jorge answered, "Not yet. First, I have to convince the employees to join an advocacy group to help the Amazon rainforest, and then I will talk to my father. I have to leave now."

The blue macaw nodded and flew way above Jorge to investigate what he was planning. As he walked back to his father's farm, the notorious farmer was having a snack, greedily eating Pao de Queijo (cheese rolls) far away from all the other people working on his farm. Jorge walked up to the employees who were eating lunch. Jorge spoke up, "Hi, I come here to speak for the trees and animals."

As soon as Jorge spoke, everyone started laughing. The boy was blushing from embarrassment. He sucked up his embarrassment and spoke up, "I come here to speak to you all, for a good reason! Cutting down trees and burning our rainforest will have serious consequences to all of us. We must stop this now before it is too late!" The blue macaw listened to Jorge's wonderful speech but felt the loss of his chicks, nest, and home even more. Now was the time for him to avenge the loss of his chicks by helping the Amazon rainforest. As his speech went on, his father kept on eating more cheese rolls, not even listening to any of it. Once Jorge finished his moving speech, only twenty out of about two hundred employees joined.

The twenty employees and Jorge went to nearby cities and told everyone there about the destruction of the Amazon rainforest. The blue macaw followed Jorge as he went to a bustling city. Jorge was nervous at first, but gradually started to speak more confidently. He truly was a natural speaker. Nearly everyone agreed to join his advocacy group. Once Jorge assembled a group, the blue macaw flew down to him and said, "Fantastic speech Jorge! Now what will you do? Convince your father, perhaps?"

Jorge replied, "I was thinking of posting my speech on social media to have a bigger impact. I already asked each member in my advocacy group to tell all their friends and spread the message. Once more people in the entire country and even beyond become more aware of the issues, then I can tell my father."

I said, "That is ambitious, Jorge, but you can do it!"

As Jorge and the employees went back to the farm, the blue macaw flew over the car they were in. He noticed a sign that had the notorious farmer selling vegetables, fruits, and beef. Under the picture were the words, "Doing good for the world". How ironic, thought the blue macaw.

They arrived back at the farm without the notorious farmer noticing. The blue macaw went to his office and found his computer. The blue macaw opened a blank document and typed up everything a reporter or journalist would need to know about the Amazon rainforest. He added Jorge's name under the article and sent it to well-known news outlets. As soon as the article was sent, the notorious farmer came into his office. The blue macaw quickly shut the computer and flew out of the nearest window. Phew, he thought. He flew back to the rainforest and saw the place where his home used to be. The land was pale orange and dry with no streams, plants, or animals. It became another desolate part of the forest. The notorious farmer was going to move his cattle to this cleared area soon. The blue macaw's stomach started to churn as he remembered the horrid day that his poor chicks were killed. He flew beyond and saw a perfect tree to rebuild his nest in the future and start anew. At that moment, the blue macaw just wanted to sleep. He was exhausted.

As he slept, he dreamt of the future. There was no more home. The Amazon rainforest was burning with fires everywhere, and the sky was black with smoke. But then he heard something unexpected, his chicks! He flew to them as fast as he could but when he arrived, it was too late. They were just a pile of ashes. The blue macaw gasped and jolted awake, panting in panic. He remembered that he had never told Jorge about the article that he sent. The blue macaw rushed back to the farm and saw a reporter interviewing Jorge.

Jorge spoke to the reporter. "Farmers are burning down trees in the Amazon rainforest. More than two hundred thousand acres of this beautiful forest are being lost every day."

The blue macaw listened attentively as the reporter attacked Jorge with questions.

The blue macaw admired how Jorge diligently answered the reporter's questions. It was like a never-ending game of tag. Finally, the interview ended. To the surprise of the blue macaw, the reporter entered the notorious farmer's house and asked him if he could feature the interview. Now Jorge's father knew all about it. The notorious farmer replied, "I will think about it."

The notorious farmer came hastily out of the house. He yelled, "How could you betray me! How could you betray the farm! You are a disappointment! You are no longer my son." He left without letting Jorge speak. Jorge began to sob. How could his father be so cruel? The reporter was still there but pretended not to notice the fight. The blue macaw flew over to the notorious farmer and yelled, "You do not know any better, do you? Destroying the Amazon and profiting from it are your only goals, right? Never say that your son has disappointed you because the truth is that you have disappointed him." He flew away and could see the father speechless, full of sorrow and regret. Then the blue macaw saw the farmer turn to the reporter and signed the consent form to feature the interview on the news channel. Certainly, the notorious farmer was a good person deep down.

The next morning, thousands of people gathered around the farm in response to their televised interview. They were going to help save the forest. They stood on land that was going to be burnt down by farmers to raise cattle. There was a farmer with his employees trying to pass through to burn down the Amazon rainforest. People protested, holding up their signs that said, "Save the forest" or, "Stop deforestation." Jorge was front and centre. Watching from above was the blue macaw, perched on a high branch.

Then something unexpected happened. The notorious farmer walked towards the group holding a sign that said, "The Amazon matters." Jorge's father said to his son, "I am sorry about what I said. You were right. I was a horrible person, so I am deeply sorry son." Jorge let go of his sign and hugged his father, "Thank you, dad! I love you." This was a scene the blue macaw could never forget. A beautiful family fighting for the same cause.

Twenty years later...

The blue macaw flew above the Amazon rainforest and admired how beautiful it had become in the last twenty years. Everybody had helped to repair the damages. Trees were flourishing, growing to even greater heights than ever before. The sky was blue and bright. Jorge and his father were more united and happier than ever, after defending the wonderful Amazon rainforest. Laws had been introduced that protected the land of Indigenous peoples and prohibited burning land, chopping trees, and poaching. Despite the laws, there remained selfish people who continued to illegally chop down trees, but more guards were protecting the Amazon rainforest: the lungs of the world!

The blue macaw saw a tree full of fresh Brazilian nuts. He grabbed four. He flew to his nest and saw his beautiful baby blue macaws. He fed each one a nut as he heard them chirp, story, story! Now was the time for his babies to hear about their father's legacy and dreams of a better future. A future of love, peace, and continuous protection of the rainforest and environment.

The Hope of Khannone

Lily Abibi Malaika Namata, Malawi

H ere is a story you have heard before, passed down by generations. Told by some, yet understood by few. This is the story of Khannone, a young, poor, African girl from the small nation of Malawi, the warm heart of Africa, who overcame the societal norms set by her ancestors, to make a positive impact on all those she met. From breaking the rules set by society, to inspiring her fellow girls from her home village in Kada.

Here is her story...

Born on 6th July 1905, to parents that were controlled by the British colonizers, from the long hours and low wages, her parents simply could not afford to feed an extra mouth in their household. Yet despite this, Khannone brought nothing but joy into the lives of her parents. She had a smile that radiated like the sun, which greatly complimented her dark complexion. Although they lived in dire poverty, Chisomo and Rejoice Mtonga, were determined to ensure that their daughter never had to worry about when her next meal would be. Just like all parents, they wanted to see their baby girl grow up to become successful. This dream only lasted for two years. The two parents went on to have seven more children, which was custom for African families. As a result, money was spread even thinner. Times became tough. Food became scarce. The family struggled.

Growing up, Khannone idolized the girls she would read about in her books. They were all the same: blonde hair, blue eyes, freckles. Girls who got to explore the world. Khannone knew from an early age that she was special, that she would bring hope back to her family and all those in desperate need of financial aid. Of course, her parents encouraged her dreams, what type of parents would not? This was until she turned ten, the financial state of her family began to worsen, with each new child being added to the family, poverty consumed her family. The whole family would go days without eating. As a result, her parents sold her away to a wealthy older man, who would go on to impregnate her, at the early age of twelve.

Her family recovered as a result, but this marked the end of her journey. She became her husband's property. No more school. No more freedom. Now her days would be consumed by caring for her daughter, cooking for her husband, cleaning the house, going to the market... activities expected to be carried out by women. For the next two years, this is what consumed her life. An endless monotonous cycle that had no end. For days on end, Khannone would weep, pleading to God to deliver her from the dreadful crisis that she had been forced to live through. In many ways, she wished to live in a world that did not objectify women and sell them off at the convenience of the family. She hoped for a future that would treat her like the African princess she wished to be.

Khannone had never made it past primary school. She was barely able to read or write, which meant that leaving her husband was never a possibility as it would leave her alone in the world, and most importantly, bring shame to her family. As in many cultures, women were expected to be obedient and submissive to their husbands, regardless of the situation. This led Khannone, the young mother, to go on and bear two more children, all before the age of fourteen. This entrapment caused great distress for Khannone, with each passing year, as she brought a new life into this world, she would pray that her children, her daughters, would not have to endure the abuse she was forced into. This led Khannone to name her daughters, Kuwala, which means to shine, and Limbikani, which means work hard, each child mending the broken heart of their dear mother. It was through her daughters that she would find the strength to persevere and overcome her situation.

In April 1920, Khannone was sent by her husband to the market to buy vegetables for the evening meal. As she walked through her usual route, she was met with the gruesome screams of a young woman from the house opposite the road. As Khannone walked towards the house, she was met with the horrific sight of a man continuously hitting a young woman, who was no older than herself. As blood coursed out the girl's body, the man stood up, spat down on her, and simply walked away, leaving the poor girl to die on her own. This did not sit right with Khannone. She patiently waited for the man to disappear out of sight before climbing through an open window. Rushing towards the girl, Khannone said a quiet prayer under her breath, pleading for the girl to continue fighting. Khannone had never seen this girl before, she was new to the village. As Khannone rushed to her side, it was clear the girl was gone. She had been beaten to death. Khannone rushed to the local police, who were found a kilometre way from the household, yet to her surprise, the attending officer behind the desk was the same man who had beaten the girl. In fear of meeting the same fateful end, Khannone turned away and continued on with her journey, not forgetting the tragic events of the day. As the days passed, she learned more about the girl, whose name was Violet Banda. Khannone learned that Violet came from the neighbouring village of Lujeri. She was the new wife to the commanding officer of the local police, who ruled her death to be a result of a break-in, trying to cover up the truth.

This showed Khannone just how unfair society was, as she had witnessed how men had complete power over women. Khannone knew that she could not live with herself if she were to ever hear of another young woman meeting the same tragic end. Although she could not save Violet's life, she was determined to save the lives of other women in her village, as it soon became evident to her that such circumstances were not uncommon. The previous year alone, three thousand five hundred women were raped, yet only twenty men were arrested for the assault. These statistics created a void in her heart. Nevertheless, there was nothing that Khannone could do, she was forced to live with the memory of that treacherous night, bearing the burden of the violence she saw. Days turned into weeks, then months, then years, with rape cases continuously on the rise. Even so, no action was being taken.

Consequently, Khannone lived in continuous fear that her poverty-stricken life would have the same fateful end, as with each passing month, her husband, Moses, became increasingly violent and abusive towards her. With his broad shoulders, skin the color of cocoa powder, Moses was an exact representation of an African giant descending from the Maseko clan, who controlled and ruled the village for as long as people could remember. Although he was a man of power, there had been moments in their marriage where Khannone loved her husband, times when he would treat her like an African queen, who deserved the world, and nothing less. He was not a bad man, she never believed so, he was just confined by societal expectations, which forced him to develop a toxic masculine personality. This is what she believed would be the downfall of the village, as she believed that there would come a day where the tables would turn, and chaos would break out, creating a rift between the people.

Little did she know that she would be the one to bring this change.

Although she had never attended secondary school, her husband taught her how to read and write basic Chichewa, and on some occasions, English, which was perceived to be the language of the colonizers. Khannone had always been a quick and eager learner, hence, she was able to grasp what her husband would teach her. And in no time, she would often spend her free time reading stories in the newspaper; stories of the raging world war, the spread of deadly dangerous diseases, and the heightening political tension amongst leading developed countries.

Usually, she did not pay much attention to these events, until she read of the story of Josephine Harrison, a black woman from Sierra Leone, who fought for women's voting rights, tackling societal backlash and setting up women community programs that were aimed to empower women. In under a year, these programs educated over two thousand women, who set up small local businesses, enabling them to leave their abusive marriages, giving each woman a new chance to life, granting women the chance to be free from the shackles of gender norms. This came with severe consequences, as men saw this to be a direct attack on their pride. The women who gained the courage to branch out were forced to eventually return to their marriages, pleading and begging for their husbands to take them back, degrading themselves for the benefit of their husbands. Sadly, Josphine ended up becoming a joke within her community, driving her away from her home nation, in fear of her life, as the men's antics began to become increasingly rabid. Josephine Harrison disappeared from the public eye and was never heard from again.

This inspired Khannone to follow Josephine's footsteps, by setting up a self-help group for women, a place where they were able to come together to seek help and advice from their fellow women. This group created a safe and friendly environment that aimed to empower women and provide emotional support for all those experiencing domestic abuse, whilst also providing funds for women who were in great financial distress. Although at the start of the group, there were only ten members, by the beginning of the following year, membership had risen to over two hundred women, who came from villages across the district of Mulanje. Khannone made sure that the group did not overstep any social boundaries, in fear of meeting a fate like Josephine, and with time, the men of the community began to accept the change in female independence in the village.

Khannone taught the people of the village the importance of equality, especially in times of financial crisis, where the male had the upper hand; she showed people how having an equal society could greatly help families, as it could provide two sources of income for a family, creating stability. And with this, the village environment improved greatly. With more girls in secondary school, and fewer child marriages, the economic state of families improved.

Khannone lived to the age of forty, due to labour complications that ended up claiming her life. The Lhomwe name, Khannone, means miracle, and surely our Khannone lived up to her name, as she strived for change, as her legacy was never forgotten as her two daughters went on to expand their mother's self-help group, to reach women across Malawi, and eventually the neighboring countries of Zambia and Mozambique, spreading their mother's idea of equality in poverty.

We live in an uncertain world, a world filled with pain, hatred, and despair. As people, the least we can do is ensure everyone has the same rights, to create a fair and just world, creating a safe environment for everyone.

My Reality

Tasheni Gladys Tembo, Zambia

G uys! Hold on a minute, wait a minute, guys! This is not a movie nor is it comedy, this is my life, the life I'm subjected to, I did not choose this life but it chose me. This is "MY REALITY".

I'm about to write this huge exam, right, called GCE (General Certificate of Education). It will determine my future, guys!

So, I'm up at ten p.m. to study and "Boom!" the electricity supply is cut and I'm in darkness. I guess I can't study now! This has been going on for a while, sometimes electricity supply is cut for as long as six to eight hours a day but nowadays it is ten to twelve hours a day. Bad right? But this is my reality.

This so-called load shedding is killing me! You are probably wondering what "load shedding" is, let me explain. In our country, load shedding is when electricity supply is rationed due to the overload on the primary power source. It is used to relieve stress on a primary energy source when electricity demand is greater than the primary power source can supply. Talk about stress, I'm stressed because I can't study for my exam, so what is going to relieve my stress? Enh!

I'm going all cookoo on you guys with these scientific explanations, right? Well, let me put it in simple terms, my country depends on Hydro-electricity, meaning electricity generated from a water body, in our case, Lake Kariba. It is one of the Seven Wonders of the World, if not, it should be because it is the biggest man-made lake. Come see for yourself, very spectacular!

Come to think of it, I wonder why my country does not generate Hydro-electricity from the Zambezi River. This would help generate enough electricity supply to supplement the supply from Lake Kariba. By the way guys, Zambezi River is home of the famous Victoria Falls also known as "Mosi o Tunya" meaning "the smoke that thunders" in our local language. It is definitely one of the Seven Wonders of the World, it's amazing, and guys you should come check it out.

Anyway, the way I see it, by the time I'm thirty years old, there won't be enough electricity supply to operate my clothing industry. I mean, our country's population is growing rapidly, there won't be enough electricity supply to meet the demand. I'm just saying, but if my clothing industry is not operational my country's economy will lose-out, because I have brilliant ideas that could generate a lot of revenue for my country. I'm just thinking, why can't my country invest in other renewable energy sources such as wind, and solar power, since it is clear that my country promotes green energy in order to protect our environment. Guys, you may probably be wondering what "renewable energy" is, right? Well, it is energy that comes from natural resources or processes that are constantly replenished. For instance, water, sunlight, and wind which keep raining, shining, and blowing, even if their availability depends on season, time, and weather. This is what put us in this load shedding predicament in the first place, if we don't have enough rainfall then there won't be enough water in Lake Kariba to generate enough electricity. Anyway, that's just my thought, back to my reality.

Guys, I'm so excited, it's the day of my exam. As usual, I wake up at three a.m. to switch on the water heater before the electricity supply is cut. I'm ready for school as well as the exam, I walk six km to school. Don't ask why, of course my parents can't afford to buy a vehicle, even if they could, they cannot manage to pay for fuel with these escalating fuel prices. So, I'm forced to walk six km to and from school five days a week, and believe me guys I get so exhausted that I just want to collapse. Sad right? Well, this is my reality.

If only there was equal economic opportunity for all, but in my country, I see the rich getting richer and the poor getting poorer due to economic inequality. You see guys, our country practices the capitalist market where the wages for jobs are set by supply and demand. Currently, there are many workers willing to do a job but very few jobs. Crazy, right? But this is my reality, which is why I want to start my own clothing industry. If only there were equal distribution of wealth. If only my country could empower its citizens not only with specialized skills but also by financing their projects and businesses. This is just my thought right, anyway, back to my reality.

Guys! I'm seated in the exam room and the teacher is passing through distributing exam papers. Then all of a sudden, I hear a loud groaning sound coming from the inside of my stomach. I didn't know what to make of it at first. Am I too excited? By the time I opened my exam paper, I realized that wasn't the case. So, I opened the exam paper right, read the first question right, but could not remember the answer. Don't get me wrong, I knew the answer but I just couldn't remember it. Honestly guys, I wondered what was happening to me, then all of the sudden, like a flash bulb, I realized that I was too hungry to remember the answer to the question. Yes! Guys you heard me right, I was too HUNGRY to remember the answers. I didn't eat breakfast, not that I did not want to, it's just that we didn't have any. My parents can only afford to feed us one meal a day, and since we all leave the house in the morning and come back around five pm, my next and only meal for the day is at five pm. Yes! You heard right, one meal a day every evening. Unbelievable right? But this is my reality.

Please don't misunderstand me, it's not that my parents want or enjoy giving us one meal a day. I personally see how this affects them psychologically and emotionally, I bleed for them. It's just that the cost of living in our country is extremely high. My father is a businessman but lately his business hasn't been doing so well due to the general increase in the prices of goods and services in our Country. My beautiful mother, whom I very much look like, is a hard-working, dedicated police officer whose salary has never been increased despite the high cost of living. She still receives a meagre salary which does not meet her basic needs. If only my country could diversify its income generating sources and make effective fiscal policies which can help fight inflation. I know right, two major words here. Well, let me explain what they mean. "Fiscal" is used to describe something that relates to government money or public money, especially taxes. Whereas "inflation" is the rate of increase in prices over a given period of time.

My country's main source of revenue comes through the export of copper. We are one of the largest producers of copper in Africa. However, we are not benefiting from it due to weak fiscal policies. We should diversify our source of revenue, maybe invest in agriculture, there is a wide market out there for agriculture products. We can also try the manufacturing industry. We have enough raw materials in the country. Guys! Honestly, why import a simple thing such as a toothpick, we have enough material to produce them. Now you see why I want to establish my own clothing industry? Anyway, this is just my thought, now back to my reality.

It's March 21st, 2024, I won't forget, my exam results are out. Guys! This is what will determine my future. I have mixed feelings though. I don't know whether I can say I'm happy or simply scared because both are giving me the same vibes, the groaning in my stomach. But I'm sure I ate this time, trying to avoid a situation where I faint when I see my results. Well, guys, here goes, I open the envelope and guess what! My future is ruined, gone! I didn't make it, thanks to load shedding, exhaustion, and hunger, things that could have been avoided if my country implemented the sustainable development goals. Don't ask me what that means guys, I don't have the energy to explain.

The Lost Dream

Mohammed Al Zayegh, Gaza Palestine

In a small city in the Gaza Strip, near the beautiful smell of the sea, Ali lived with his small family. Like a small bird that dreams of flying high in the sky, like the small grass waiting for the rain to grow or the sun waiting for the day to shine, he dreamed of going to medical school to become a doctor and help his country. Ali studied hard to get the highest grades and worked diligently to create a positive impact on society. He began his studies in Gaza's Western schools and spoke to his classmates about his dream of enrolling in medical school.

When he started eleventh grade, he felt that he was so close to achieving his goal. But on a Saturday morning in October, he woke up to the sound of rocks and bombing. The schools closed, and life started to darken because of the brutal conflict in the Gaza Strip. Most schools had been destroyed. Ali held on tight to his school bag and felt his dream slip away because of the destruction of the war. He was displaced with his book, thinking he would wake up to do his lost exam, but the war raged on. He continued his lessons for as the poet Mahmoud Darweesh wrote, "Stand on the edge of the dream and fight." Here, Ali fought for his dream.

When Ali slept, he dreamed of a city filled with people who lived in peace and safety, and of a magic wand that would make wishes come true. He imagined that the wand could end the war in Gaza. He mourned the lives lost and wished to keep all the children safe. With one wave of his wand, he thought, he could fill the sky with twinkling stars and a beautiful rainbow of hope.

In the light of the stars, he wished to stop the war, and for peace to come true but he watched as the children continued their journey to heaven. The bombing of schools left him heartbroken and full of fear. When he woke up, he did not find the wand, it was a dream. Although he had no magic wand, he remembered that nations across the world worked together to create goals for the future that they would achieve together, including UN SDG 16, the goal for peace, justice, and strong institutions.

Despite the psychological exhaustion from the war, Ali would not surrender to this painful reality. He decided that he would try again and again to complete his studies and achieve his life goal. He was patient like a lone flower waiting for a bee, a desert waiting for rain, or a shadow waiting for the sun to set.

On a night when fear and loss surrounded him, he fell asleep. While sleeping, he talked to the little twinkling stars, waiting for big stars to let them shine and enjoy the company of the moon. The little stars asked him about his sadness and why he was distracted. "I lost my dream and hope of success," he said.

The little stars told him to plant a flower seed, take care of it, and write in his diary about the new plant. He dashed to the plant's pot and started to write his notes every day. He watched the flower grow every day, and it became more beautiful. A month later, the stars returned; they saw him more optimistic with his pink flower, and they felt happy with him too. They danced and had fun together. Suddenly, he woke up from his beautiful dream; he shrugged over what was happening in real life. He hurried to bring a seed to plant the flower and started caring for it. He learned that he would remain sad if he only thought about negative things. So, he would have to hold onto hope to achieve his goal.

He picked up his crayons and started to draw his little flower; it looked like it was lonely. He continued to draw flower after flower until he drew a bunch. The flowers looked happier together. He decided to plant more flowers. Tomorrow, the sun will rise, he said.

A few days later, the conflict halted, and the war stopped in his beautiful coastal city. Days began to recover from their pain, and life almost returned to normal. As a bird sought freedom, Ali ran, jumped, and shouted, "I will return to school."

Down the Ages

Carlos Andres Olivera Caballero, Bolivia

The day breaks with ominous sounds, and an atmosphere of foreboding fills the air. His father talks about the earth sweating—an indication that the sun has deserted it. The suffocating atmosphere adds weight to his words as if it were preparing itself for what was about to happen.

His dreams are haunted by a woman dressed in red, wearing a green blindfold and pursued by a fox. Her picture remains in his mind, an emblem of the fight they were going to have. Wake up, his mother tells him; there is movement everywhere in town. He sees a sign like "chilijchi" from his window, feeling like a chick sheltered but aware of dangers out there. The sky appears dangerous and birds are restless, signs that they will lose their freedom soon. Seeing Sacaba uplifts him. It is indeed hope amidst tension. He swears today he would fight for freedom, something that his family will always stand for regardless of what happens today.

His family is melancholic. His mother combs his sister's hair while his father says there will not be any food today. The chuño is scarce, and his pockets are empty. The sheep are gone, and the children's hunger is loud. The town suffers from shortages as trucks are blocked so supplies cannot reach the population. His father gives him a staff to carry, which symbolizes their community's burdens. They will stand all day, waiting for the scorched earth beneath their feet to burn in testament to our resilience.

It is a dust-filled morning. It feels like the atmosphere weighs down on us with the anticipation they have collectively built up in our hearts. Men with jaguar voices join us as families march behind them together with others whose voices resemble those of peccaries and jucumaris. Their presence both reassures and intimidates him as it reminds him of their collective strength. In this air hangs a fierce unity – that shared determination which keeps them bound together in one purpose: moving forward. Millions were mentioned by an old man but he sees thousands of reasons to go ahead because every face in the crowd tells a story, represents some kind of struggle or embodies hope for a better future. They are heading towards Huayllani bridge and its name grows louder inside him showing how important this journey really is. That is when he notices a baby's face peeking out from an aguayo, understanding for the first time that this fight is about everybody's family, not just his own.

As they approach their destination, the streets are becoming wider. On Huayllani Bridge, a symbolic and literal place of crossing stands where they will congregate in their fight. Sacaba families, and others from nearby communities wait for them. At the bridge, people begin to move slower before finally stopping there as a line of men blocks it off. These people stand in their way making it impossible to enter into the town as stipulated by law. They stay silent while deafening their shields against begging.

Their leaders hoped for a peaceful entrance that comes only with the rumble of steel beasts. The pressure builds up, and the crowd's noise gets louder. The foundation of this wall is laid by someone above who says we cannot pass through here. He hears whispers about danger and sees guns that can take away their breath. Tear gas rains down like seeds thrown from poison trees causing disorder everywhere. The choking smell envelops the air with coughing voices filling it too; it is filled with acrid fumes that make people cough and scream in pain. He catches sight of his father and mother among those present. His father's head is bleeding. He picks him up and carries him towards safety just as an ambulance arrives at the scene. Sounds of sirens mix with the noise around reminding them how dangerous this life has become.

His mother is relieved when she sees the ambulance but she is exhausted. His sister is scared but safe. Her wide eyes reflected the chaos and fear all around them and he took refuge in a nearby building. The windows show them what is happening outside. Hell is breaking loose out there. People are running, stumbling over the fallen. Stones and burning tires fill the air. Crowd members counter white tear gas with black smoke. The scene outside depicted utter chaos that resembled a battlefield where hope clashed with despair.

He sees his father's head, red with his injuries, and his mother crying helplessly, usually so strong, now with desperation in her voice. He raises his father up and tells his mum to take him to hospital. The van takes his father away while he stays and assists other people. There is so much smoke and violence but in the Whipala, unity and hope lie. A new chant of courage fills the air as a reminder of how fearless they should be.

He goes around offering assistance to anyone he can within the large crowd. To see such an evil: many were exhausted and fell or had their upper body wounded. Every face is narrating the story of a sufferer that speaks volumes of the barbarity of the day. He chances upon individuals jogging with despair and panic in their eyes. The green-uniformed men approach and rush further, contributing to the confusion and panic. Their presence is a constant and vivid threat, a reminder of the power they are dealing with. Last night, he was able to follow the rest and seek comfort within a structure which is also home to the others. The cruelty he witnesses is shocking. He sees police use violent force against unarmed civilians. The sight evokes feelings of anger and helplessness.

Hernán, a man of great courage, suffers an injury but the gleam in his eyes leaves the door to hope wide open. After picking Hernán up, he goes to the bushes but finds Hernán's blood all over his hands. Hernán expresses himself with the use of Whipala and the significance of its symbolism. The medical practitioners try their best to bring Hernán back to life, on the way to the hospital, and hope that he wakes up from that final disaster. The hospital is filled with people in agony.

His father is bandaged, and his mother takes care of him. She stays strong and cooks for him even though she is hurt too. Sadness and bitterness hover in the air. After sunset, they start to feel the pain and hardship. Tensions between the authorities and the population have escalated. People across the country are killed and injured. This is also evidenced by the presence of the Whipala, as the people continue to struggle for their rights. The colours bring out the light against the dull grey of the day reminding the people that there is always hope and strength amid the struggle. He embraces his sister and reassures her that they will keep on struggling for what they deserve. Her body shivers against hism a stark image of the child-like nature that they continuously try to shield from the world.

It is by no means the end. They will continue to be in the front lines, taking up the fight for their dignity and this equality. There is a long way to go and with all the obstacles and adversities that are sure to come their way, their spirit is unyielding. At night they huddle together in unity, souls oppressed yet spirit unbroken. In the face of such a crisis, the community would come together and find the strength to face and overcome a day that shall remain etched in their collective memories. They will keep on struggling for their own right, for those of a loved one and for generations yet unborn.

Night brings a semblance of calm, which is short lived, as the sting of the day's events are too close to heal. The hospital is a dark place where the patients lie in pain moaning and the unexpected loved ones are crying. All these people have their unique stories. As he eats dinner with the family, he is lost in deep thought of Hernán and the other individuals who sacrificed themselves. It is true, they are trail blazers and light the way with courage. And yes, this is not just a fight for oneself, one's families or even the country but their future too.

The Whipala flies and soars and remains a testament of unity and hope. The Whipala represents a dream, a dream for a better world. Those who believe in giving a voice to the voiceless are here to stay.

They leave the hospital while dawn lingers, and the city suffers in silence. There are feelings of hope, pride, and true belief in pictures of making a difference, too. As they walk down the streets, their heads are held high, ready to carry on fighting. This is their home, and they are going to defend it no matter what.

Though the journey has just begun, they are ready. Whatever lies ahead, it shall meet them—united in their quest for justice and equality. Here is where they must be: on their feet strong and beside each other for a better tomorrow. They will stand unshaken in heart and unbroken in spirit. With each step they take onward, their collective strength within comes out. They move forward, not just for themselves, but for future generations, for the hope of a world where justice reigns and equality will no longer a dream but reality itself. They are the epitome of resilience, and even though the journey may seem difficult, it is necessary for a brighter, more just future. Standing together, they are unstoppable, and their fight for a better tomorrow will echo down the ages.

The Future We Want

Tyra S. Nettey, Liberia

Leekpele Kanoway, Lee for short, is an eighteen-year-old girl who resides in the town of Folubah, Northern Liberia. Lee was an orphan who stayed in a mud house with a friend's family. She lost her parents during the fourteen-year Liberia Civil war that took place when she was six years old. Araba's family raised Lee like their own child over the years because they were good friends with Lee's parents. They tried their best by sending her to Dolokeleng Community School where she learnt only the basics. She left school after grade six dueto the constant relocation of her foster family. There was always flooding during the rainy season which caused them to evacuate their current home.

Lee and Araba are smart and beautiful young ladies who love God and worship Him wholeheartedly. They both became sisters and they assisted their parents in all they did whether it was a tough task or not. They could only afford to eat one meal a day so they worked hard every day to ensure stability instead of going to sleep hungry. In Folubah, the new town they relocated to, those who could afford it went to the town square to buy food and clean drinking water from the outer regions. Those who could not afford it, like Lee and Araba's family, were forced to work on the farms of people just to get four pieces of cassava or yam at the end of the day. There was a creek down the hill not far from town where these people fetched water for drinking and cooking while some were washing, bathing and even excreting. This was the means of survival for the poor people of Folubah.

During the dry season, many crops were cultivated and this was the time the workers looked forward to. They would receive double of what they usually got and have sufficient meals. Lee's family often ate in excess during the dry season but they came up with a plan to sell their excess food to other workers and use their money to buy products from the town square. They wanted to live healthier during that time instead of living extravagantly.

At the town square, there were two queues; one for the poor families who only came to buy during the dry season and the other for their regular customers. They were victims of discrimination. The rich thought they were better than them due to their hard standard of living. The sales women would even make them stand in the line for a long time while they served everyone on the regular customer line before serving them.

Weeks passed and the people were back to their poor standard of living where they ate one meal and drank creek water. This time around Lee's family was the only exception. They still continued to drink clean water and eat nutritional food but not because they were now rich but because Lee and Araba had been learning trades and skills from the sales women at the town square. They would make brooms from palm trees, weave baskets, make attires for children from banana leaves and even help with some medicinal issues so whenever they returned home, they practiced these skills until they were great at it.

People came from the lower part of Folubah to buy some house materials from these girls and that is how they were earning enough to constantly buy from the town square. With these little earnings, Lee and Araba started to build a much better house with sticks instead of mud that would not be affected if flood came. They doubled up their game to quickly finish the house before the heavy rains came.

Rumour had it that Lee and Araba were their town's richest residents at the time. People in town began whispering about the possibility of the girls joining the higher authorities in decision-making. They thought it was a great idea because they would be of big help due to the outward trade connections the girls had made with their customers. They concluded that the clans and paramount chiefs must be in awe of them upon hearing the news of their work so they set up a meeting with the town's higher authorities where this request was brought to their attention with excitement. The chiefs declined it immediately. They told the girls that they were foolish for thinking they would be accepted to partake in decision-making and other higher affairs. They made it well clear that girls had no place or position in authority because it is only fit for men to lead and women to submit and follow. These men were misogynistic pigs and never willing to change.

Regardless, Lee and Araba continued their trade and they grew bigger and better with more external connections. Their soaring success was widely spread across neighbouring towns and Araba's father was a proud man who thanked God every day for the children he had raised. They were now living a little above the normal standard of life of the people of Folubah. Then the time came when Araba was of age and men were to ask her father for her hand in marriage. There were many suitors but she rejected them all because men from that town were misogynistic. She wanted a man who valued equality in all forms and dimensions. She was focused on making a change in their neighbourhood and helping out those who could barely afford to feed themselves. She wanted to build a school where all children could attend whether poor or wealthy, boy or girl or even smart or slow to learn.

Lee and Araba decided to redevelop their town little by little by getting all the help they needed. They taught other women the skills they learned while men were involved in the distribution of the goods they had in stock. These men also learned how to make charcoal from large forest trees and tap wine. With this availability of opportunities for almost everyone in the town to work and earn, Folubah was gradually being rebuilt. There were no longer mud houses across the lands, no unclean creek water for consumption and at least two meals a day in these homes. The people thanked Araba and Lee every day for making this way of life possible and continued to ring praises of them throughout that year.

Mr. Wehjay Tetteh, one of the biggest businessmen in that region, met with the girls and from the discussion they had he admired how they were both spiritually and physically strong. He then offered them a deal to be business partners to take their trade to the next level. He encapsulated their profits and the percentage they would get from these distributions. The girls discussed it briefly with their parents, neighbours and workers present that day. They took the offer and signed a paper Mr. Tetteh gave them to seal the deal then business started effectively and immediately the next week.

Mr. Tetteh and the girls reached the apex of success in due time. He admired their hard work and intelligence to strategize and innovate to boost their business. With consistent incomes and profits, Folubah saw a reduction of prices of the items sold at the town square so everyone could afford to buy nutritional food for good health. Over time, they were able to dig wells and hand pumps for clean and safe water for consumption. Soon enough, everyone in Folubah would be as healthy as the governmental families.

Mr. Tetteh then suggested to Araba and Lee that they should continue their education so that they would be respected by higher authorities from across the regions. People who were uneducated were rarely given opportunities to be a part of the larger society. Lee and Araba thought it wise and decided to further their studies while continuing their business. Mr. Tetteh offered them a place to stay whenever they came to his town where they were enrolled in fully facilitated schools. Lee dreamt of being a doctor while Araba wanted to be a tutor. They both took classes relating to their ambitions. They also helped their peers enrol in school. Lee and Araba were both brilliant ladies so they undoubtably excelled in their academics and business. Their parents were proud.

A few years later, it was the girls' graduation. Finishing high school at the age of twenty-nine was not a common or easy thing to do but Lee and Araba did it. The children of Folubah looked up to them and gradually started following in their footsteps.

The next step was to attend university to achieve their goals but not everything comes easily. Universities were built in outer regions and people who could afford to attend were dignitaries and influential families. With all the earnings Mr. Tetteh and the ladies saved up, it still was not enough to pay for tuition at any university but Mr. Tetteh did not give up. He had now become a father figure to Lee and Araba and he wanted them to be able to give back to their community and society. He sought help through external connections he had but they were all dead ends until one fine day he got an invitation to African Dreams University in Southern Liberia.

Two days after receiving the invitation from ADU, Mr. Tetteh arrived at the university. He met with an old friend, David Royce, who told him he was only able to get a partial scholarship for Lee and Araba. They would have to pay half of the tuition fees in order for them to attend. He thanked Mr. Royce gracefully and headed back home to share the good news. Lee and Araba were so grateful to Mr. Tetteh for all the help he was continuing to give them and they prayed to God for long life so he could reap the fruits of his labour.

After finding a way to double their earnings to pay for the half tuition, the ladies trained others as their replacements in the business.

In Duport Road, people lived in fancy houses unlike Folubah. ADU was situated in the middle of Duport Road and it was easily located. Lee and Araba stayed at the almost abandoned dormitory of the school as partial scholarship students while the fully paid students stayed at the well-built dormitory. Students from Dorm A did not associate with students from Dorm B because they claimed to be better than them and referred to them as Slum Rats. They ate separately, played sports and even congregated separately. In classes when lecturers asked questions, the Dorm A students were given the chance to answer before Dorm B students which gave them low marks in class participation. That is how the school has been for years. Lee and Araba found it difficult to adapt despite doing well in their courses but they had no other option but to play by the rules. They both made new friends and even formed a group called Students Equality Council where all students were respected and given the privilege to participate in any activity they had. This made a lot of Dorm B students feel like they belonged and less angry about the class discrimination which went on for years.

The years of studies finally paid off and the ladies, Araba and Lee, were both living their dreams. Lee topped her class throughout the semesters which made her a student of honour so she was given a job at ADU hospital (the biggest hospital in the region). Araba on the other hand became a facilitator/tutor/mentor and was offered a position to teach at Duport Road's High School. Both ladies were finally living the dream they had just a few years back and they thanked God first, Mr. Tetteh second then the people of Folubah including their parents.

At Duport Road High School (DRHS), Araba was a tutor and mentor to all the students. Carefully studying the classroom teachings, Araba noticed that there was discrimination among the students. She wanted to make a change in the shattered and broken school system so she scheduled a meeting with the principal of the school on the elimination of the discrimination in the classroom. Everyone deserves an equal point of view on lectures in classes. Being a partial scholarship student does not mean you should be treated poorly. She was not going to let history repeat itself so she stood up for the students.

It was the first day of the week and Araba met with the principal of DRHS, Mr. George Tarpeh, to discuss how to put an end to the day-to-day division made in the school and unfair treatment students got. She pleaded with Mr. Tarpeh to put a stop to it. Mr. Tarpeh promised he would gradually put an end to it. But in fact, he was the one who brought the idea of division of students and giving them lesser privilege to participate in lectures and other activities of the classroom. Why would he end it now?

Weeks passed since the meeting with Mr. Tarpeh was held and nothing changed. Araba then decided to take the next step by reaching the administration of the school to let them know Mr. Tarpeh was ruining their school with unjust acts like the discrimination in the classes. If word got out about this, people would stop sending their children to the school due to bad reputation. Mr. Larbie heard the rumors of Araba's meeting with the administration and he threatened her to step down.

Furious as a lion, Araba explained everything that was happening at the school and how Mr. Tarpeh had threatened her. Lee told her to do what was right and not back down until a change was made and Mr. Tetteh also told her that he would report a case at the police station concerning Mr. Tarpeh's threat.

Feeling at ease the next morning, Araba went on to meet with the administration and made them aware of the deeds taking place in the school and how to put an end to it. They immediately called Mr. Tarpeh in and suspended him indefinitely for the unfair and unjust actions he carried out in the school. Araba replaced him as acting principal for that year and she made sure that all students were given equal rights and privileges to participate in any activity both in and out of the classroom. She paid visits to other schools to carry on awareness of equality among students whether wealthy or not. She was certain to make this change in the shattered systems of schools.

Lee also took a stand at work to stop the injustice and unfair treatment people got from these influential families. Everyone was supposed to live in harmony and peace but also with dignity and justice in every aspect. Back at Folubah, Araba along with some of the people who were now working at good job sites built a school where all children from that region could attend to get quality education. Lee also had partners and sponsors who helped her build a well facilitated hospital and few clinics where people got treated properly from diseases and sicknesses. Other people who also had external connections and partners helped construct buildings and build roads for good means of transportation.

Folubah was now a town with a hospital and clinics, a school where both men and women could teach, buildings, a reservoir, wells and hand pumps and affordable food for all. This development gradually spread across the regions and soon enough, Liberia was a well-developed country.

Lee was invited to speak in a media conference for Eastern Liberia. She chose her words carefully and struck to the truth: "We are survivors of war, hardships and poverty. Our lives back in the day were difficult and some of us could barely afford to eat twice a day. We had dreams and no matter what happened, we strived to achieve them. Little children look up to their parents or family and even people in their surroundings to determine how their future will be. A farmer's son would want to be a farmer like his father when he grows up because that is all that he knows. This mode of mediocrity needs to stop in order to have great future leaders of this generation. There should be no form of corruption or injustice in our settings. These government policies against corruption should be static and not biased. We are the only ones who can develop our country and enable sustainability in every aspect of our lives. I tell my life story to inspire youth to make change the world. This is the future we want and we won't stop till we achieve it".

The press took note of her vision and courage, reaching thousands of others to advance change for more sustainable development across Liberia.

The Dream of Fatima

Sanika Addri, United Kingdom

Fatima closes her first job at the clinic. It was a busy day for her as many people were injured from the earthquake. She changes into a different uniform and goes to her second job. She has three. She needs them so she can achieve her dream. "You are late again!" her boss, Rakesh tells her. "Sorry, I had to treat the people who were injured." Her boss gets a bit cross. "This is your last chance!" he tells her and points her to her work.

Fatima gets on with her work without complaining because she knows she cannot say anything. She needs this job to fulfil her dream. Fatima's dream had always been to open clinics across Bangladesh, especially in areas that had poor access to health-care. In those regions, if someone got sick, they would have to travel miles before they could reach a hospital. She wanted them to have a hospital near their home. She did not want them to have the same experience as her sister who died because there was no clinic close to their home.

She finishes her work quietly and after her work is over, she changes her clothes again to go to her third job. She gets there and starts working immediately. Her other boss, Firoza is nicer and supports her in her dream. But she does not have much income. She finishes her work and Firoza gives her some food to eat. Fatima thanks her and gets up to leave. Firoza calls her and gives her an envelope. Fatima opens it and she sees that there is money inside. "What is this? No, I can't accept this." Fatima tries to give it back. But Firoza does not take it. She insists that Fatima takes it because she wants Fatima's dream to come true as soon as it can. Fatima goes home and saves the money for her savings for two years. She recounts the money, and she still has a long way to go.

A few days later, she arrives at her clinic a bit late, as she got caught up in job search-ing after being fired by Rakesh. She arrives at her clinic and sees it getting destroyed. She runs to the people standing in front and asks what is happening. They tell her they saw a Facebook post that this clinic gives fake medication. Confused, Fatima asks herself "Who could do something like this?" She looks behind and sees Rakesh. She immediately knows it is him. Rakesh never wanted Fatima to follow her dream. He thought it was useless and he did not think that Fatima could ever achieve it. "Why did you do this? I never hurt you, did I?" Fatima is furious. "Well, I want to remind you that your dream is worthless so you should give up," Rakesh replies. Fatima storms off. She runs to her house and locks herself in.

She is devastated. She does not know what to do. It took her so much work to build that clinic and she was one step closer to her dreams. Now, she was pushed a step back. Someone knocks on her door. It's Firoza. "It's going to be ok, Fatima. Just hang in there." For the next few months, Fatima works even harder. She finds more jobs and saves more money now. She even moved as she could not find many jobs in that area. She does not know if all her hard work will pay off. But she does it because she knows it will take her closer to her dream. Her dream is also the dream of many others. Her dream will be helpful to many people around the country. She is determined to help people.

After earning a quarter of her goal, she decides to rest for a bit so she comes back to her village. While she is walking home, she sees many cars in front of Firoza's house and she gets confused. This is the first time she had ever seen cars around this place. Firoza comes out, looking very excited which makes Fatima even more confused. "Fatima! I've been waiting for you. Come inside." Fatima goes in and sees that there are many people. So many that it was hard for Fatima to find a place to sit. "After what happened with Rakesh, I talked with a distant relative and he used his connections to get to these people. They would like to help you. They want to help you make your dream come true!" Firoza tells her.

Fatima is shocked. She cannot believe so many people want to help her. One man comes forward and introduces himself. "Hello Fatima! It's great to meet you. I'm Mr. Akash and my team would like to help you achieve your dream. We will take care of the expenses and you will do the rest. But you must prove that you deserve our help. You have to work hard and not look back. Don't let anything or anyone get to you, ok?" Fatima nods. She invites Mr. Akash and his team to discuss her plan. They observe her plan and suggest some changes to make it even stronger.

With a strong plan and a strong team behind her, Fatima is now even more confident in achieving her dream. She starts to set up clinics. Firstly, she sets one up in her village, this time, a bit far from Rakesh's house. She then travels to other villages near her village and sets up a clinic on each. It takes up all her time and her strength but she is patient. She prepared for this for years and since it is coming true, she will not back off.

After setting up two clinics, there comes a challenge. Some people do not like how she is building clinics in their village, Shanta, because it is taking up space where they want to build shops and farms. People in the village start arguing about it and tell her to shut down her clinic. But she knows she cannot give in.

She later calls a meeting in the village with every villager so she can convince them. She discusses why it would be good to have a clinic in their village and how it would make things easier. Still, some people were debating against her. But she did not give up. She showed more reasons and gave real-life examples of how a few days ago a pregnant woman in Shanta died because it was too late when she was taken to a hospital that was far away. Everyone then agreed so she continued. She built a clinic in that village and then moved on to another village.

Fatima was happy. She was happy with her progress and she was happy that her dream was finally coming true. But what she did not know was that more challenges were coming up. When she started setting up clinics in Khulna, the weather and climate were very different. The ground and soil were different as well, so they needed different types of supplies. And that meant more money was needed. Fatima calculated the new cost with Mr. Akash, and it was much over their budget. Mr. Akash suggested that they skip some areas of their plan, so they do not exceed their budget. Fatima disagreed. Her dream was to set up a clinic in every rural area there was not one before. And she is determined to accomplish it. "I will arrange the money somehow. We can't stop now." She says so Mr. Akash agrees. They keep on with their work while Fatima goes back to her village to arrange more money.

She takes the last savings she had in case of emergencies and counts the money. She still is a bit short. At first, she does not know what she should do. Then she thinks about whether she should borrow some money from someone. She could not think of anyone at first. But then, she thinks of Firoza. She does not know if she should ask her as Firoza herself does not have much money. But she knows Firoza would love to help so she runs to her house and asks her if she can borrow a few thousand Tk (Bangladeshi currency). Firoza does not hesitate. She trusts Fatima. She looks for her savings to give Fatima but still, there is not enough money. She calls her relatives and borrows money from them and gives the money to Fatima. Then she wishes her good luck. Fatima thanks her and travels back to Khulna, where Mr. Akash and his team are. With their new budget, they start working again.

It takes time, a lot of time. Years to be specific. Buildin clinics in many areas is not an easy job. But it does not matter to Fatima. She will not stop. Finally, after four years of hard work, Fatima finishes setting up the last clinic in Banshkhali. But now there is something else to think about.

All this time while they were building the clinics after a clinic was built, someone from Mr. Akash's team used to run it. But now they will not be here anymore, so Fatima needs to find doctors and nurses for the clinics. She goes to the nearest hospital from every clinic and asks if they have some doctors who can volunteer to work in the clinic for some hours. Thankfully, most hospitals had doctors who were happy to volunteer. But she still could not find enough doctors so there was no one to work at Banshkhali. Fatima does not know what to do. She could stay here herself, but she also had a clinic back in her village.

Then she gets an idea. She calls Firoza and asks her for help. She asks her to find someone who can work at the clinic in her village while she works here. She plans to work here until someone can take over this clinic so she can go back to hers. It was hard but fortunately, Firoza found someone who could work at the clinic temporarily while Fatima works at Banshkhali. After a year, someone finally volunteers to take over the clinic in Banshkhali so Fatima can go back to her clinic. But before, she visits all the other clinics she built in the different areas to see how much people are using them. To her surprise, there were way more people than she thought. And that made her very happy. After that, she went back to her village and started working in her village.

After all her hard work and determination, she finally achieved her dream. Her dream of everyone having access to adequate healthcare. But she could not have done it without someone's help. That someone knocks on the door of her clinic. She goes and opens it and smiles when she sees the person. It was Firoza. The friend who supported her with everything from the start. Firoza comes in and Fatima gives her an envelope. "What is this?" she asks Fatima. "It's a thank-you gift for all your help and support," Fatima tells her. It was an envelope full of money and Firoza was happy to receive it. "What now?" Firoza asks her. "Maybe I'll try to open clinics and hospitals around the whole world." Fatima smiles. She knows how clinics are needed not just in Bangladesh but in many other countries as well. "Just need another person like me to do it." Firoza laughs.

They both know it and we all know it. How the world just needs some people to raise awareness and open some clinics for people so that everyone can maintain their good health and well-being. We do not need to open hundreds. We do not even need to open one. But trying to raise money for one is also something we can do. It might look little, but if everyone does something little, then eventually it becomes something big. The future depends on the present so let's make it beautiful!

The Promise

Tasnim Lamine, Morocco

The sea was raging when the migrant boat arrived at Dakhla. It was hard to believe they had escaped death. They had left their home country to escape famine, poverty, and injustice, and now faced an unknown future in Morocco. They hoped for a brighter future.

Two years later, a child was born to one of the immigrants who had married. They named him Amadi, which means "the free man". It was not easy for migrants to find work and the majority of them collected waste, including Amadi's parents, doing the impossible to provide for their son. Amadi grew, reaching the legal age to enter school. He was eagerly awaiting the moment but soon discovered racism and was bullied by students at school. Lonely and unable to express himself, he was ridiculed by others. They called him Azwa which means "the Black". They bullied his skin colour and his accent. Although he was Moroccan, his original accent from Senegal shone clearly. Amandi found his comfort in front of the sea sharing his worries with the waves. His parents collected waste there. His attention was focused on the amount of waste that polluted the sea almost as if the sea has problems and concerns too. From his great love for the ocean, he often tried to organise clean ups. However, one child's efforts were not enough. The pollution increased day by day, until the boy vowed that he would save the sea and the environment from pollution. "I'll save you, I promise, my friend," he said.

One day, his teacher entered the classroom and asked the students to pay attention quietly and then said "I have big news for you. I have created a new school club for addressing environment issues." Most of the students ignored the news because they did not care about environmental problems, in fact they were contributing to polluting it. During the break, the students went out to the school yard and while the teacher was watching the students, he saw one of them throw a plastic water bottle on the ground. Amadi took the bottle and started transforming it to a submarine, the teacher was surprised by what he saw and Amadi's talent he approached him. He was blown away by his creativity. The break was over, so he took his hand and they went to the classroom. Then the teacher said to the class "Look! Your friend took the bottle you littered and transformed it into a submarine. Give him a hand!"

The teacher encouraged Amadi to join the environmental club. Amadi was ecstatic. Some students began talking to him and he started to build friendships. They soon became a great team. One day, the teacher announced that there would be a national speech competition with the theme of climate change and protecting the environment. Amadi did not forget his promise to the sea. This would be the opportunity to share nature's voice. The team worked day and night to make their region Dakhla proud. They chose to talk about the future of renewable energy in Dakhla. The competition was tight but after a hard fight, they won first place nationally with three awards: the best team, the best project, and the best leader for Amadi.

After their victory Amadi became well known at his school and received great respect from his peers. He became active in school clubs and he got his confidence back. He impressed people with his thoughts and creativity in the development of his country and the achievement of a successful future. In his junior high school and high school, he represented his community and participated in many competitions and debates about climate change and human rights. Although he moved to other schools for his studies, he stayed in touch with his teacher who helped overcome his shyness and helped him become one of the most creative and distinguished pupils in Morocco.

Amadi strived every day to achieve his goal to protect and defend the environment and he hoped that his voice would be heard for the whole world to hear so that he could convey the suffering of the environment and work to find solutions to it. One day, came across an opportunity to work with the United Nations and become a Youth Climate Justice member. He did not hesitate to fill out the form and two months later, he was accepted.

Amadi stood now in front of the United Nations assembly. He began his speech, "Mr. President and representatives of States, I stand in front of you today to speak on behalf of the environment and mankind. It feels just like yesterday when I first complained to the sea. The sea listened to me without getting sick of me, and even more so, it endured me, even though it was steeped in his concerns. I ask myself why a person might let the sea suffer from pollution. While it listens patiently to our complaints, we let it down every time, failing to protect it. We don't care about its fate. I remember my father talking about our home country and praying when they emigrated from it for fear of starvation, poverty and injustice. My parents came from a city that had no sea. They would not have hesitated to drink from this sea or any sea that they could find, despite its salinity, so as to avoid drinking water that is almost black from pollution. I am here to convey to you the suffering and the voice of countries whose inhabitants have not attained the most basic rights to live and the voice of people who are subjected to violence, racism, discrimination and contempt. It is not for man to be white, black or red. Everyone in our world has a role to play and no creature whatsoever to diminish it."

"Gentlemen, do you know how many people have died because they have been exposed to this pollution? We have always dreamed of a world free of all injustice. All people are equal, whatever their colour, race, religion or form. We want to end poverty and hunger in all their forms wherever they may be. We want to build societies whose first goal is to protect human rights and we want the children of the whole world to learn.

It is a fundamental and natural right. Just as human have rights, the nature in which we live must also have rights. My name is Amadi which means the free man and I will fight for the rest of my life until all humans are AMADIS!". Everyone applauded they were impressed by his spirit of struggle. He also thanked them for their support and encouragement to him.

Amadi decided to visit his primary school and he was greeted by the teachers and the director of the school. Amadi did not forget the memories there and thanks to Amadi, his school was transformed into an ecological school through the project Dakhla Smart City. He wanted to return the favour to the city and the country where he was born and raised. At the end of the day, he visited his friend, the sea. He saw that the beach and the sea were clean, he sat down watching the waves and said "I didn't forget my promise, here I am sitting again in the same place to tell you that I'll do the impossible to defend your rights, sea, you see?"

The Leaves of Hope

Shyam Manikandan, India

It was a beautiful morning. The sun was shining through the sage green leaves of the thick forest, and the birds were chirping as they fluttered in the foliage. The gentle rustling of leaves mingled with the sounds of the creatures of the forest, a peaceful moment rich and biodiverse.

In a small mountain village close by, Arun and Padma were getting ready for school. "Mama, you forgot to pack me food!" shouted Padma waking Arun from his slumber. "Coming dear, I have packed your favourite food foxtail millet and some dough balls made with mountain honey," replied their mother. "Seriously Mama, why do we always have to eat this? Why don't you allow me to buy cupcakes which are wrapped in colourful plastic packs from the canteen instead?" Arun asked. His mother replied, "No Arun; this is the same food our ancestors consumed and lived happily without contracting any diseases. You must have healthy food too." She handed Padma and Arun their packages wrapped in banana leaves. "Now go, otherwise you will be late for school. Bye, bye!" said their mom. "Bye mama!" replied the siblings.

They exited their thatched straw hut to find their best friend Aarush waiting for them. "Hi Aarush, are you ready to go to school?" asked Padma. "Sure, let's go" replied Aarush.

They started walking. "Walk fast. We still have eight kilometres of climbing to go in order to reach school", said Arun. Soon, they entered the forest. They had all practically grown up in the forest and knew almost every living being.

"Did you hear that a tiger had entered the village last night and attacked the goats in the goat pen? The shepherd told my mother this.", said Aarush. "Oh no! When a tiger attacks a village, it keeps coming back until it is caught.", said Arun. "Do you know the reason for this tiger attack?" asked Padma. When no one replied, she answered, "I read in a school library book that loss of habitat pushes tigers out of forests and into villages. Did you know that tigers have lost ninety five percent of their historical ranges, all destroyed by deforestation?"

"Okay, so what is the solution for this?" asked Aarush. "Reclaiming the forest land by afforestation," replied Padma. "And how do you do that?" asked Arun. "With this," replied Padma as she took out some seed balls from her bag. She then explained how it was made. "This seed ball is made from clay, compost and seeds. When I throw this ball in the soil, the seed will germinate into a sapling, then a plant and finally a new tree is formed," explained Padma. "Why is it made out of clay?" asked Aarush. "The clay is used for protecting the seeds from birds and ants and the compost provides nutrition until the seeds germinate," replied Padma. "Wow, that's a great idea! Can you teach me how to use it?" asked the boys. "Sure! I learned this technique in the school workshop and I can teach this to all the children in our village," replied Padma. "Will this workshop be free?" asked Aarush. "Of course, it is. After all, our mother nature provides everything for free," said Padma.

Their discussion came to an abrupt stop as they heard loud tapping sounds deep inside the woods. Padma whispered "Shh.... everyone" and they moved slowly towards the sound taking cover in the bushes. To their surprise, they saw a group of five people cutting the trees. "They are teak wood smugglers," whispered Arun. "Teak wood is moist, light and heat resistant. It is not damaged by pests and other harmful agents. Known for its durability, it is the preferred choice for construction of villas among wealthy people. Teak trees are endangered and are protected by the government authorities and cutting them is a punishable offence. But smugglers take advantage of the wide forest area to hide and smuggle out the tree for a huge sum of money," he continued. Suddenly, one of the smugglers turned suspiciously and started heading towards their hiding spot. It seemed that he had spotted them. The children were paralyzed in fear. In a flash, however Padma jolted them back to their senses and pulling their hands, fled. As they turned back, they could see all the smugglers chasing them, shouting "You will be silenced, and suffer first!"

They used all their courage and speed to get away. They did not say a single word till they reached the school. They knew it would be dangerous to interfere with smugglers all by themselves, as warned by their parents. They were unusually quiet in the class, sunken in their own thoughts, barely listening to the math teacher. This went on for few months. The math teacher instantly understood that something was wrong. She demanded, "Padma, I know that you are physically present here, but is your mind here? Can you solve this sum for me?" Padma could not solve the problem and stood blank. Soon after the class, the teacher said, "Padma, meet me in the staffroom during break."

The science class went on without any problem and after that, it was lunch break. Padma had no mood to eat her lunch. Still with her sunken spirits, she reached the staffroom. To her utter surprise, she found Arun and Aarush also standing there along with the Headmistress. She thought, "Looks like they both have also been caught for their lack of attention in class!"

The Headmistress gently asked, "What happened to you today?" I heard from the teachers that you were very restless in the class. Hope everything is well?" Melted by the softness of the Headmistress's tone, Padma started weeping and blurted out the whole story. The headmistress consoled them. "Dear children, you are all brave. I am very proud of you. Did you inform your parents?" "Yes, ma'am, they are aware of it, but they told us not to interfere with the smugglers as they are dangerous people," said Arun. Aarush added, "We want to save the trees. They are our friends and protectors on our way back and forth to school. We do not know what to do. Kindly guide us." The headmistress replied with an assuring voice, "Do not worry. The district collector is visiting our school next week to raise the flag in our celebrations on Republic Day. You all can meet him at that time and request his support." Padma jumped in excitement, "Thank you ma'am!"

Later that evening, as Padma and Aarush were completing their homework, an idea sparked in Padma's mind. "In advance of the collector's visits, we can raise awareness! We can tell everyone about the dangers of deforestation and how important trees are."

Aarush's eyes lit up. "That's a great idea! We can hold a campaign in the village!"
The three friends spent the next few days planning. They decided to name their campaign "Save Our Trees." They collected information from their school library about deforestation, its impact on the environment, and the importance of planting trees. They practiced speeches and made colourful posters using recycled paper and natural dyes instead of normal paper. Padma, with her knowledge from the seed ball workshop, decided to make seed balls with the villagers. They gathered clay, compost, and native tree seeds. Padma patiently explained the process. Soon, the villagers were rolling seed balls too. The day of the campaign arrived. The village square bustled with activity. Padma, Arun, and Aarush stood on a makeshift stage, their hearts pounding with a mix of nervousness and excitement. Padma, the bravest and most articulate of the three, took the lead. "Dear friends, relatives and elders!" she said, her voice ringing out across the square. "We stand here today because our forest is in danger. Teak wood smugglers are destroying our trees. This means they are destroying us and our future!"

She spoke about the role of trees in maintaining the ecological balance, providing clean air, and preventing soil erosion. Arun followed, explaining the impact of deforestation on wildlife and the danger it posed to the village itself. Finally, Aarush taught them all how to make seed balls and explained their role in restoring the ecosystem through reforestation. The villagers listened intently; their faces concerned. Many of them had witnessed the reducing area of the forest but did not know the seriousness of the situation. Padma's speech woke everyone up.

The campaign was a huge success. The villagers pledged their support to "Save Our Trees." They also convinced others to stop buying products made from illegally smuggled wood and to actively participate in tree-planting initiatives. With the help of the villagers, Padma, Arun, and Aarush flung hundreds of seed balls throughout the forest and even along the roadsides creating a wildlife corridor. News of the children's campaign spread like wildfire. Local newspapers and television channels picked up the story. Soon, their efforts gained the attention of environmental organizations who offered their help.

Next month, the district collector visited the school, and the headmistress arranged a meeting with the three children, as promised. The district collector was kind enough to understand their plight and appreciated their attempts to bring the truth to light. He immediately called the forest department officer, highlighting the problem. He assured the children that the government officials would be taking action with immediate effect. He also said that the role of youth is very essential to save forests. He declared Padma as student ambassador for this project. Reassured, the kids went home happily.

A few months later, on their way down to school, Padma noticed two tiny leaves peeping out of the soil in the same area where the bare cut trunk of the old teak stood. She greeted them with tears in her eyes.

Balanced Light, Balanced Life

Myat Pan Khit, Myanmar

In the apartment complex in the heart of Yangon City, lived a young girl named Sandar. Sandar was a curious child, always seeking new adventures, even within the confines of her home on the fortieth floor. Although she could not play outside as much as she wanted due to the long distance to the nearest playground, she always found joy in the little things brought alive by her vivid imagination.

From the balcony, Sandar often gazed down at the world below, imagining herself as a giant from Jack and the Beanstalk, watching over the ant-like people scurrying about their daily life. Same days, she would lie on her back and stare at the sky. The clouds became her canvas, transforming from fluffy white shapes into majestic dragons and soaring eagles.

One time, she even spotted the shape of a giant lion battling a majestic peacock in the sky, a sight that filled her with excitement and wonder.
"Mom! Look! There is a huge lion fighting a feathered, fierce peacock! The peacock is about to win!" Sandar pulled her mother's hand, excitedly pointing at the drifting clouds in the morning sky.

Her mother smiled tenderly at Sandar. She could not see a lion or a peacock in the sky but she did see two shapes colliding with one another in the clear sky.

"I am sure they are, Thamee," Her mother replied. "Now let's hurry up. Your friends are going to play without you if we don't arrive soon."

"No! Let's go. I want to play htoe si toe with them! I will show them how fast I can be!" Sandar declared, eager to win in htoe si toe, a traditional Myanmar game where people have to pass through the borders without being tagged by the other team. Sandar enjoyed playing it because it was the only game where she could win. Her small stature allowed her to quickly sneak past the borders and earn a point, much to her friends' chagrin. They often bemoaned how unfair it was but enjoyed playing as much as she did. Sandar ran quickly, dragging her mother behind to get to her school like Nga Htwe Yu, one of The Four Paladins.

As much as Sandar enjoyed watching the clear blue sky during the day, she did not enjoy staring at the night sky. To Sandar, the night sky was boring and lifeless. It was not pretty, nor was it decorated with numerous interesting shapes and objects. Instead, it was pitch black, all foggy and blurred.

Many people including her teachers, her parents and the characters in the story books exclaimed that the night sky was adorned with twinkling stars, accompanying the elegant moon in the vast space. But that was not true. Every time she looked at the sky, there was only a smudged moon, lonely in the sky. Sandar felt sad every time she saw it, especially because she was named after the moon. If the moon had to be alone for eternity in the vast sky, did that mean Sandar had to live a lonely life too?

One morning, during breakfast, Sandar could not keep her thoughts to herself any longer.
"Daddy, why is the moon always alone in the sky? Do stars not exist anymore?" she asked, her voice tinged with worry and her little face scrunched up in confusion. Her parents exchanged a glance. Her father put down the newspaper he was reading, while her mother scooped extra rice into Sandar's father's bowl.

"Oh, of course not, darling. The moon is not as lonely as you might think, you know?" her father said, smiling at her mother as in gratitude.

"What do you mean? We never see stars at night."

"But there are stars in the sky. We just don't see them because all the buildings in the city are so bright that they block the natural light from space. It's a phenomenon called light pollution. You have learned about pollution at school, right?" Her father began to draw long blocks and rays of light on the empty side of the newspaper to explain the concept.

"Yes, we learnt about pollution at school. It's something that's harmful to us and our environment like our water and our air. But why aren't we stopping it? The books say that pollution is bad for nature and everyone needs to do their part to prevent it. So why don't we take action about light pollution? Is it because light pollution has no side effects like water or soil pollution, daddy?"

Sandar's dad shook his head at her question. "No, of course not. Light pollution can have negative effects on human health, such as disrupting sleep patterns and increasing the risk of certain diseases."

"It also has significant impacts on wildlife too," her mother added. "Imagine a flashlight pointing at you while you are trying to sleep. It hurts your eyes and makes it difficult to fall asleep, right? The same goes for animals in the wild who rely on darkness for hunting, hiding, and other essential activities. Light pollution can throw off their entire ecosystem and put their survival at risk."

"Poor animals..." Sandar murmured, feeling a pang of empathy. She touched her eyes, imagining how exhausted the animals must be feeling.

"That's correct," her father continued. "And it's not good for the cities either. Because we have to supply tons of energy to light up the entire city, a lot of fuel and money goes to waste. If we reduce light pollution, we can save energy and reduce our carbon footprint, which helps combat climate change."

"Carbon footprint is the total amount of greenhouse gases we add to the atmosphere, right? The gases that keep the Earth warm."

Her father nodded and said, "But too much of these gases means the Earth gets too warm, causing natural disasters, and contributing to global warming."

Sandar's eyes widened with determination. "Then we need to take action, daddy. Children like me should learn more about this and help make our city a better place. Maybe we can turn off unnecessary lights at night. We don't need all the lights for the entire city at night when we have the moon and the stars. We should have them at the dark corners of the streets and roads though. Many villains attack people at those places and people might get hurt."

"That's a great idea, Sandar. You can start by sharing what you've learned with your friends and teachers. Education is the first step towards making a difference and you can inspire them to make a change," her mother encouraged.
Sandar nodded with determination, looking ready to get out from the chair and run to the school.

"But not now. You need to finish your breakfast." Sandar wilted at this but started eating her breakfast quickly. Her parents shared a smile at their daughter's eagerness. They knew that she would tackle whatever challenges came her way in life with the same determination and courage.

That day, during the lunch break, instead of persuading her friends to play htote si toe, Sandar gathered them all around and told them about the disappearing night stars, the light pollution and its negative effects.

"What can we do, Sandar?" asked her friend Su Su, her eyes wide with concern.

"We can start by turning off lights when we don't need them," Sandar suggested. "And we can talk to our parents and teachers about it. We can even have a special night where we all turn off the lights for an hour and look at the stars."

Su Su's eyes sparkled with excitement. "Let's call it 'Lights Out Night'! We can make posters and tell everyone in school!"

As they brainstormed ideas, another classmate, Zayar, raised an issue. "My grandma lives in the countryside and they don't have enough electricity. They have all the night skies, but it's unfair that they live in darkness while we have too much light in the city. Since the city has enough electricity to power the buildings all night, maybe it could help provide the village with more electricity."

Indeed, life in the countryside was beautiful and peaceful, yet it lacked modern conveniences like electricity. Every time Zayar visited his grandmother, he enjoyed running in the fields, helping his uncles fetch coconuts, and exploring the vibrant village. The days were filled with the sounds of nature and the laughter of children playing. However, it was the complete opposite at night. The village, so full of life during the day, became dark and unsettling.

Without electricity, the nights were pitch black, save for the faint glow of the moon and stars. This lack of light made it difficult for children to read books and for adults to continue their work or socialize. The villagers relied on dim, flickering oil lamps, which were not only insufficient but also posed fire hazards. The darkness hindered the village's potential to thrive, affecting education, safety, and overall quality of life.

Sandar's eyes lit up with a new idea. "That's a great point, Zayar. We can talk to the city council about both reducing light pollution and helping villages like your grandma's get the electricity they need."

Her friends nodded in agreement, excited about making a positive impact in both urban and rural areas.

The next day, the children approached their teacher with determination. They explained how they wanted to address not only the light pollution in the city but also the lack of electricity in the countryside. Their teacher was impressed by their thoughtful approach and agreed to help them spread the word. The children spent days making colourful posters practicing speeches for their campaign. The principal even allowed them to make an announcement during the morning assembly.

Their message was simple but powerful: reduce light pollution in the city to save energy and help rural areas gain access to electricity. They called it "Balanced Light, Balanced Life."

On the day of the city council meeting, Sandar and her friends stood nervously at the entrance of the council chamber, holding their posters and notes. Their campaign had caught the attention of a city politician who invited them to talk and share about their work in front of the council.

Sandar felt a mix of excitement and anxiety as she prepared to speak, knowing that this was their chance to make a real impact on local policy decisions. The room was full of politicians, council members and reporters, all eyes on them as they took their place at the podium. Sandar took a deep breath, feeling the weight of responsibility on her shoulders, but also a sense of determination to make their voices heard.

Sandar stepped up to the microphone, her heart pounding. She took a deep breath and began, "Mingalar par shint. My name is Sandar, and today, I want to talk to you about light pollution..."

She spoke passionately about how light pollution affected not just the stars and the moon, but also human health, wildlife, and the environment. She then added, "But while we reduce light pollution in the city, we must also help our countryside. My friend Zayar's grandmother lives in a village where they don't have enough electricity. And it's not fair that they have to live in darkness while we waste light."

"We believe that by reducing unnecessary lights in the city, we can save energy and redirect it to rural areas that need it more," Sandar proposed. "Not only will this help bring back the stars to our night sky, but it will also improve the lives of people in villages like Ko Ko's grandma's."

Zayar added, "The countryside is beautiful, but the lack of electricity makes life difficult. With better lighting, children can study in the evenings, and adults can work and feel safer at night."

Their friends shared their thoughts and experiences, explaining how they had started turning off unnecessary lights and encouraging others to do the same. They also advocated for providing sustainable energy solutions to rural areas.

By the end of their presentation, the room was filled with applause. The council members were impressed by the children's dedication and thoughtful approach. They promised to consider their proposals and look into ways to reduce light pollution while also supporting rural electrification projects.

As they left the council chamber, Sandar felt a surge of pride and hope. She knew that they had taken an important step towards making a positive change. And maybe, just maybe, the night sky would soon be filled with stars once more, not just for her but for everyone to enjoy.

Years passed and the city had slowly and steadily decreased the number of artificial lights in the night sky. The city had implemented measures to reduce light pollution, such as installing shielded streetlights and promoting energy conservation. Moreover, resources were allocated to the countryside to improve their access to electricity through sustainable means such as solar panels and wind turbines.

That night, Sandar stood on her balcony, looking up at the sky. She gasped in delight. The stars had appeared, twinkling brightly around the moon. She felt a sense of achievement and pride. The moon was not lonely anymore, and neither was she. Zayar's grandmother and the villagers did not have to live in the darkness and the stars did not hide in dismay anymore.

As the stars shimmered, Sandar knew that she and her friends had made a difference. They had helped create a sustainable future, one where both people and nature could thrive. And she realized that this was just the beginning. She hoped that one day everyone could admire the night sky without having to wonder if the moon was lonely like her. She hoped that one day animals and people did not have to suffer anymore. And she hoped for balance between the city and the country, bringing better life quality for all.

From Arid to Eden

Mary Adwo Ansah, Ghana

It was a long and tiresome effort as I trudged through the dusty landscape, my own thirst and exhaustion mirroring the desolation around me. The sun beat down relentlessly, draining the last drops of energy from my exhausted body. I had been searching for water for hours, but every step seemed to lead me further away from my goal. The ground was parched and cracked, the earth dry and withered. With each step, my surroundings remained eerily consistent. It had been two years since the last fell and my life was shaped a barren land, devoid of any plant. I am Kolawale Junior, and this is the story of how drought ravaged my community.

As I approached my house, I could not help but feel a sense of despair wash over me. The once-blooming garden in front of our compound was now a mere shadow of its former self. The trees had withered, leaving behind a trail of dry leaves that crunched under my feet. The windows of our small mud-brick house seemed to stare back at me like empty eyes, a constant reminder of what befell us.

I entered through the front door, my legs heavy with exhaustion. My mother, Yaa, looked up from her seat on the floor. "Kolawole my son, how was your search?" she asked, her eyes filled with a mix of concern and resignation.

I shook my head, feeling the weight of her question bearing down on me. "It was fruitless mother, we found nothing but dust and dry earth," I replied, my voice barely above a whisper.
She nodded, her eyes dropping to the floor. "I feared as much. The drought has taken everything from us."

I collapsed onto the floor beside her, feeling the hard, dry earth beneath me. We sat in silence for a moment, the only sound being the creak of the old wooden moving door due to the gentle breeze. Then, I spoke up, audible and firm this time around. "Mother, I can't help but feel that there must be a way out of this. A way to restore our land to its former glory."

Yaa looked at me, I could see a hint of a smile on her lips. "You have always been a dreamer, Kolawole," she said. "But sometimes, even dreams are not enough." I looked at her, determination burning in my chest. I refuse to give up, Mother. I will find a way to bring life back to our land, no matter what it takes. My journey to find a solution began at that very moment.

The next day and the few days that followed, I began scouring the village for clues, talking to everyone I came across and searching for any hints that might lead me to a solution. But every door I knocked on, seemed to lead to a dead end. The villagers were either too defeated or too sceptical to offer any hope.

It was the last day of the month, a time that young people my age would gather to discuss age grade matters. During these meetings, some community issues were also raised for discussion, the issue of drought being the primary subject.

"Today's meeting was quite brief," Adesun our spokesman said as we exited the village Town Hall, which we traditionally called Usor (meeting place).

I first nodded in agreement. "We didn't have much to say since we haven't figured out a solution to our water challenge yet," I replied as I adjusted my short to enable me bend to pick up my chewing stick, which had fallen while I nodded in response to Adesun's statement.

The day was still young and there was a lot to accomplish. I remembered I had to visit Edi, my best friend, who was having a child naming ceremony the next day and needed my help. I quickly parted from Adesun, heading to Edi's place. I did not even move up thirty paces when I noticed someone sitting at a mud building few metres away from me. It was a new building and judging from how polished the clay wall looked, I could tell the building had just been erected some days ago.

Sitting at the front was a man, whose face was buried in a long scroll, surrounded by a small pile of books and papers. On getting closer, I recognized him, Baba Akoto, a wise elder who had spent many years studying the ancient ways of our people. I approached him hesitantly, not wanting to disturb him. His eyes still fixed on the scroll. "Good afternoon, Baba," I said giving a slight bow.

He looked up, giving me a quick stare before speaking. "Kolawole, my young friend, how are you today?" he said, his voice low and soothing.

"Very fine baba," I said, my voice barely a whisper as I ran my eyes through the first to last writing on a book cover with the title "Famine". He could see the intensity of my stare on the books and the eagerness to ask him a lot of questions.

"Speak Kola" he urged immediately, dropping the scroll after he was done writing a statement on the fourth line. I began asking him questions about the community's current predicament
Baba drew out a book from the pile of books on his left side.

"You see Kola," he began and that was how I learned of the way that our ancestors had built elaborate systems to harvest and conserve water.

As I listened, a spark of hope ignited within me. I realized that the answers I was seeking were not new ones, but ancient ones that had been lost over time.

"Baba Akoto," I said, my voice filled with excitement. "Do you think it's possible to rebuild these systems? To bring life back to our land?"

He looked at me, his eyes twinkling with a hint of mischief. "I not only think it's possible, Kolawole, I know it is. And it is very, very necessary."

Speaking with Baba, I forgot my errand to Edi's house! The sun was beginning to fade away. I apologized to my friend the next day. I didn't have to bother about waking anyone when I knocked on the door loudly the second time because baba never got married nor had children.

We spent countless hours that day pouring over dusty books, uncovering secrets and techniques that had been lost for generations.

We began by designing traditional wooden pumps to harness the precious underground water our community never knew existed or maybe knew but were uncertain how to harvest. We also designed canal systems to distribute this water throughout the village. It was backbreaking work, but we laboured tirelessly, driven by our vision of a lush and thriving community.

As the days turned into weeks, our efforts began to bear fruit. First, we enlisted the help of the local skilled artisan, Ola. He was an expert in wood work and could turn any idea into a physical masterpiece. With the help of the villagers as well, we began to dig canals according to what we had designed. The once-barren fields began to sprout with new life as we were able to harvest this underground water. The villagers, who had initially scoffed at our efforts, began to take notice and even offer their support.

But we still had one challenge to solve. The drought had left the land without nutrients and we needed a way to restore the soil's fertility. Baba Akoto revealed to me an ancient technique, passed down through our ancestors, that involved mixing borage and fenugreek to create a potent fertilizer. The aroma that wafted form the mixture was pungent and earthy, and we knew we had created something special. We needed these plants in large quantities so as to meet the nutrient demand of the vast barren expanse of land in my community.

It was the last day of the week and the sun had risen rather too early for me. I laid still in bed thinking of how my journey would go in search of seeds for ancient local fertilising plants. Rumour had it that Amolina, a small village twelve miles away had the two crops we needed, planted in abundance. "What if it was not true?" was my most frequent thought as I set out on my journey. Baba had advised that if the plants were found, I should return quickly so as to inform our community leader. He would then reach out to Amolina to see if we could reach a deal on exchanging what we had with them in exchange for borage and fenugreek.

Our plan worked and with our fertilizer in hand, we set out to revitalize the soil. We worked tirelessly, spreading the mixture across the parched earth. And then, the miracle we had been waiting for. The soil began to heal, and new life burst forth from the ground. Green shoots sprouted ...our village was reborn!

Hope in the Dark

Charles Bonney Ghartey, Ghana

The sun had gone down behind the village Elabela, leaving a warm, golden glow that mixed with the sadness in the air. Sad songs floated from nearby huts where families gathered to comfort each other. Baby Pipo lay in his crib, unaware of the tragedy that had struck his parents. The fire had destroyed their home and taken his parents, leaving him alone in the world.

"Mema, I'm scared," Zusa signed with her hands, her eyes wide with fear, her fingers trembling.

Mema, an elderly woman with deep wrinkles on her face, looked at Zusa with compassion. She held the young girl close. "Don't worry, child, I'm here for you," Mema whispered softly, her voice calming Zusa's fears.

Outside, the village grew quiet as night fell. The air was cool with the scent of cooking fires. Mema led Zusa to a woven mat in the corner of the hut, and they sat together quietly, finding comfort in each other's presence. After a while, Mema spoke again, her voice steady and calm. "We must be strong, Zusa. Your parents loved you dearly, and now it's our duty to protect and care for you."

Zusa nodded, sadness and uncertainty in her young face. She was only eight years old and the sudden loss of her parents weighed heavily on her. Suddenly, there was a soft knock on the door of the hut. Mema looked up, surprised. Visitors at this hour were rare, especially after such a tragedy. She stood up gracefully and opened the door, revealing two figures.

One was Mama Kosi, the village elder known for her wisdom and kindness. The other was Kwamesa, a young man who had grown up with Zusa's parents and treated her like a younger sister. His strong face softened as he looked at Zusa with sympathy.

"Mema," Mama Kosi spoke gently, her voice filled with wisdom, "we heard about what happened. Our hearts ache for young Pipo and Zusa."

Mema nodded gratefully, inviting them inside. "Thank you, Mama Kosi, Kwamesa," she said, her voice thick with emotion. "Your presence means a lot to us."

Kwamesa knelt beside Zusa and placed a reassuring hand on her shoulder. "Hey there, little one," he said warmly. "I'm here for you, just like your parents would have wanted."

Zusa looked up at Kwamesa, tears shimmering in her eyes. "Will everything be okay, Kwamesa?" she asked quietly, her trust in him evident.

Kwamesa smiled gently. "We'll make sure of it. You're not alone, Zusa. We're all here for you."

Mama Kosi settled beside Mema, her expression serious yet determined. "Mema, after talking with the elders, we know that Zusa and Pipo will need our support more than ever."

Mema nodded, feeling grateful for the support of her community. "Yes, Mama Kosi. We'll do whatever it takes to care for them."

With Mama Kosi's guidance, the village rallied around Mema, Zusa, and baby Pipo in the days that followed. Neighbors brought food, blankets, and comfort. The women of the village took turns watching over Zusa and Pipo, ensuring they were never alone. Kwamesa, especially, became Zusa's protector and mentor, spending hours teaching her about their traditions and sharing stories of bravery and strength.

As time passed, Zusa found comfort in the routines of daily life. She helped Mema with chores, fetched water from the village well, and played with the other children who welcomed her warmly. Slowly, the pain in her heart began to ease, replaced by a growing sense of belonging and security.

One evening, as the sun dipped below the horizon, painting the sky in shades of pink and gold, Mema gathered the village children around a crackling fire. They sat in a circle on woven mats, their faces glowing in the firelight.

"Mema, tell us a story," one of the children said eagerly, eyes bright with anticipation.

Mema smiled warmly, her voice filled with the tales of generations past. "Ah, my little ones, gather close. I'll tell you a story of hope in the face of darkness."

And so, under the starry sky, Mema shared a story of courage and strength. She spoke of ancestors who had faced great challenges but never lost hope. She described a village much like theirs, where love and unity had overcome hardship time and time again.

As the children listened, their imaginations expanded. They imagined themselves as heroes and heroines, facing their own trials with bravery. And among them sat Zusa, her eyes shining with newfound strength, knowing she was surrounded by love. She had her village, Mema, and Kwamesa by her side.

Pipo grew up to be a curious boy who loved exploring and collecting things. He wanted to find ways to prevent tragedies like the one that took his parents. Zusa, who couldn't hear or speak, used art to communicate. She was very good at it. If she wanted to convey any message, she would draw something to depict what she is trying to say, making her exercise her talent more often and eventually improving her skills.

Pipo and Zusa spent their afternoons in the village square, surrounded by Zusa's colorful artwork and Pipo's laughter. Despite her inability to hear or speak, Zusa had a remarkable ability to understand others through keen observation and empathy. The villagers admired her resilience and creativity, often stopping by to admire her latest drawings and engage in simple sign language conversations.

As the years passed, Pipo became determined to understand the scientific reasons behind Zusa's condition. He spent countless hours researching medical journals and consulting with healers from neighbouring villages. One day, he came across an old herbalist who claimed to have insights into unusual ailments.

The herbalist, Mama Kwena, was known for her deep knowledge of traditional medicines and the human body. Pipo visited her small hut on the outskirts of the village, where she welcomed him with a warm smile and the aroma of medicinal herbs. Sitting on a mat, Pipo explained Zusa's story and showed Mama Kwena some of Zusa's intricate drawings.

Mama Kwena examined the drawings carefully, her weathered hands tracing the lines with a knowing touch. After a long silence, she spoke softly. "The fire that took her parents was not just a tragedy of flames, but of energies disturbed. Zusa's ability to hear and speak was lost not in her ears or vocal cords, but in the delicate balance of her spirit and body."

Pipo listened intently as Mama Kwena continued. "When the fire raged through their home, it left an imprint on Zusa's soul. Her spirit retreated, leaving behind the functions tied to sound and speech. But her artistic spirit flourished, finding expression through her hands and eyes."

Pipo was fascinated yet troubled by Mama Kwena's words. He asked, "Is there anything we can do to help Zusa regain her abilities?"

Mama Kwena nodded thoughtfully. "Time and understanding can heal wounds of the spirit. Take her to the forest, where the rhythms of nature can speak to her soul. Encourage her to find her voice in the silence, and she may rediscover what was lost."

Grateful for Mama Kwena's wisdom, Pipo returned to the village determined to help Zusa. He found her in their usual spot in the square, meticulously sketching a scene of the village market bustling with activity. Sitting beside her, Pipo gently explained what he had learned from Mama Kwena.

Zusa looked at him with eyes that sparkled with understanding. She embraced Pipo's idea eagerly, sensing a new journey of discovery ahead. The next morning, Pipo and Zusa set off for the forest on the outskirts of the village. The air was thick with the scent of wildflowers and the sounds of birdsong.

In the heart of the forest, Zusa felt a deep sense of peace. She wandered among towering trees, her fingers tracing the rough bark as if reading a story written in textures. Pipo watched her with admiration, realizing that nature was indeed speaking to her in its own silent language.

Days turned into weeks as Pipo and Zusa returned to the forest regularly. With each visit, Zusa's confidence grew. She began to experiment with different forms of art, from intricate sketches to vibrant paintings using natural pigments she gathered herself. Her art became a bridge, connecting her inner world with the villagers who had once struggled to understand her.

One afternoon, as they sat under a sprawling baobab tree, a group of children from the village approached them tentatively. Pipo smiled encouragingly as Zusa picked up a stick and began to draw in the soft earth beneath the tree. The children watched in awe as a simple sketch of a dancing antelope emerged before their eyes.

One brave child, named Kofi, stepped forward and asked, "What does it mean?"

Zusa looked at Kofi and then at her drawing. With a twinkle in her eye, she gestured for him to sit beside her. Using simple gestures and expressions, she told the story of the antelope that danced under the full moon, bringing laughter and joy to the village. The children listened intently, captivated by her tale.

From that day on, Zusa became known not only for her art but also for her ability to weave stories with her hands. She found a voice that transcended words, touching the hearts of everyone who took the time to understand her unique language.
As for Pipo, he continued his quest to understand the mysteries of the human spirit and the connections between art, healing, and the natural world. He documented Zusa's journey in a series of sketches and writings, hoping to inspire others to see beyond differences and embrace the richness of human diversity.

Pipo always loved Zusa's art. Her paintings and sculptures told stories about their village's history, present life, and hopes for the future. But it wasn't until a huge fire destroyed half of their village that Pipo truly understood how wise Zusa was.

After the fire, while the village mourned and worked hard to rebuild, Zusa spent a lot of time in her art hut. Pipo, still grieving everything the fire had taken away, found comfort in helping Zusa with her artwork. He watched her create scenes of nature with such detail that they looked alive – animals, plants, and landscapes coming to life under her skilled hands.

One evening, as they worked together, Zusa paused and pointed to a series of new paintings. Pipo studied them carefully, trying to understand what they meant. Unlike her usual vibrant pieces, these paintings were mournful. They showed animals running from fires, trees burning, and villagers looking helpless.

Pipo felt a heavy feeling in his chest as he realized what Zusa was trying to say. Her art showed how nature was delicate and how human actions could make natural events worse. The fires that had destroyed their village weren't punishments from an angry god, as some believed, but natural events made worse by people.

This realization sparked an idea in Pipo's mind. Inspired by Zusa's art and determined to protect their village, he imagined a device that could detect fires early and warn everyone. Together, they began working on it, combining Zusa's artistic sense with Pipo's knowledge of machines and chemicals.
They called their invention the Wildlife Fire Alarm. It used sensors placed around the village and in the forest nearby. These sensors could sense changes in temperature,

humidity, and air quality – signs that a fire might start. When they sensed danger, the sensors would send signals to the village with bells and lights, giving people time to react and evacuate if needed.

Pipo and Zusa worked hard on their invention, testing different materials and making many adjustments. They stayed up late in Zusa's hut, discussing their progress and dreaming of a safer future for their village.

After many nights of work, the Wildlife Fire Alarm was ready. The villagers gathered in the town square as Pipo and Zusa showed them how it worked. At first, people were not sure if it would really help. But when Pipo demonstrated how sensitive the device was to even small changes in the environment, people started to believe.

The village chief, an old man with kind eyes, thanked Pipo and Zusa for their hard work and clever idea. He talked about the losses the village had suffered in the fire, and how the Wildlife Fire Alarm gave them hope. It meant they could stop another disaster before it destroyed more homes and lives.

"We have lived for many years under the belief that each year the god of fire rules our town," the chief began, his voice carrying the weight of tradition. "We made sacrifices with fire, believing it would bring us a bountiful harvest. But it was a deception. We now see that true protection comes not from appeasing gods but from the ingenuity and dedication of our own people."

Over the months, the Wildlife Fire Alarm proved its worth. It detected several small fires early, so people could put them out quickly or get away safely. Pipo and Zusa kept improving their invention, making it better and more reliable.

News of the Wildlife Fire Alarm spread to nearby villages. Soon, Pipo and Zusa were traveling to teach other communities how to protect themselves from wildfires. They became leaders in fire safety, mixing art and science in a new way. Kwamesa, who had once catered for Zusa, approached Mema and other members in the community. "Do you remember how we used to gather every year to make sacrifices to the fire god?" she asked, a hint of scepticism in her voice. "It's incredible how Pipo and Zusa's device has changed our perspective. We've been living under a belief that held us back, and now we see a path forward based on real protection and innovation."

Pipo and Zusa caught their breath in the crowd. They silently acknowledged what they had achieved together. Their journey from tragedy to success had bonded them deeply.

"We did it together," signed Pipo to Zusa, his hands showing both relief and pride. "You've always been my voice, Pipo. We're strong when we're together," Zusa replied, tears of joy and gratitude in her eyes. She squeezed Pipo's hand.

The villagers gathered around them, thanking them sincerely. They spoke about how Pipo and Zusa's bravery and cleverness had brought back hope and secured everyone's future. Pipo felt fulfilled. He had not only prevented another tragedy but had also honoured his parents in a meaningful way. Night fell over Elabela, now called Hope in the Dark. The village square was alive with celebration. Pipo and Zusa were at the centre, their story now a legend among the villagers. They had turned their pain into a purpose, their sadness into a story of strength and new ideas.

In the days after, Pipo and Zusa kept working on their Wildlife Fire Alarm. They shared their story with nearby villages, making their bond even stronger with every life they touched and every heart they inspired. Every evening, as they watched the sunset over Elabela, they knew that even in life's hardest times, there would always be hope. A hope that came from facing darkness together and finding light in each other's friendship.

The Climate Diaries

Tahani Moosa Wadiwala, South Africa

Tasheni Gambi entered this world along a river bank bordering Zambia and Zimbabwe in the depths of winter's dry spell. Her elated parents had grand dreams for their newest child and out of gratitude for being blessed with a baby girl they gave her the name Tasheni, meaning "Being thankful to God".

Tasheni had a remarkable childhood, raised by her father, who was a farmer, and her mother who devoted her life to taking care of Tasheni and her three older siblings. Tasheni's parents shared with her and her siblings a love for reading and taught the importance of seeking knowledge at any age. Her siblings played a significant role in influencing her perspectives and traits, and in moulding Tasheni into the adult she was becoming. She lived a traditional Zambian childhood, which revolved around traditions, community, and a strong connection to nature. Many community members held an intense appreciation to God for creating this earth and its enchanting ecosystems.

At the young age of three, Tasheni got her first taste of widespread hunger. In 2011 her beautiful country experienced one of the region's worst droughts in centuries that led to hunger, which forced citizens to adapt to these environmental challenges. This challenged her family's income as her father's harvest was hindered and he was left with stunted crops. At such a young age, she could not comprehend the effects of this everlasting water shortage that would limit basic human needs such as access to clean water and would mark her country with a significant loss of agriculture, an increase in mortality rates and worsening the economy leading to increased poverty.

In the year 2015 at the age of seven, the Kariba power station which supplied electrical energy to Zambia and Zimbabwe was unable to provide electricity to urban and rural areas in the country, due to low water levels from the Kariba dam that supplies electricity to neighbouring nations. This led to a period of darkness and business closures. As a result, Tasheni developed an interest in understanding why her beloved country faced the never-ending hardships of continuous periods of drought.

During her teenage years Tasheni prioritized education and she took initiative to earn extra income to support her family. Like any child, she had aspirations to build a better future and wanted to be remembered as someone who contributed to the development of her country. In today's society, having access to the internet is seen as being as important as a basic human need. Living in a rural area that had unevenly distributed access to the internet disadvantaged Tasheni and her siblings but this taught them to be innovative and find ways to cope during the drought season. Despite her circumstances she managed to maintain resilience in hopes of achieving her goal to aid her country from the everlasting droughts.

As the years passed, she gained independence and would go out of her way multiple times a week to try to find Wi-Fi hotspots and internet cafes in urban areas, just so she could have access to expanding her research. From the thousands of articles that she came across regarding Zambian droughts, she understood that climate change is the driving factor behind the increased frequency and severity of Zambian droughts that occur every four to five years since 1981. This was heartbreaking news, as climate change is caused by humans and is preventable. What type of person can be so cruel to take God's gift and repeatedly commit actions to harm and abuse the planet? Persistent misuse shall inevitably lead to harmful repercussions, which is exactly what is happening in Zambia as well as countries across the globe.

This sparked Tasheni's interest to dig deeper and find out what exactly is causing climate change and what could be done to prevent the chronic droughts that Zambia faced. Community members could not understand why she was so invested in a cause like this, but the truth of the matter was that everyone was suffering, the country as a whole was suffering and no one seemed to care that at the rate of the frequent droughts, in under five decades, the country would no longer be a suitable home for its inhabitants.

The people in her circle, her peers and friends were severely uneducated on how climate change was affecting them and Tasheni felt like it was her duty to foster awareness on climate change. They were unaware that climate change is caused by a combination of human actions and natural phenomena, but we as humans can do better. We have to do better to help Zambia and multiple other countries that experience the effects of climate change.

During Tasheni's research, she discovered that in Zambia, deforestation is a significant contributor to global warming. As forests are cleared, Carbon dioxide gets released into the atmosphere and diminishes the forests' capacity to act as carbon sinks. Additionally, unsustainable land use and agricultural practices impact the local climate patterns in Zambia, which results in droughts, leading to agricultural challenges, meaning it is a never-ending cycle. Furthermore, Greenhouse Gas Emissions from activities such as industrial processes contribute to the emission of Carbon dioxide and methane, which trap heat into the atmosphere ensuing changes in the regional climate.

Climate change in the country has caused devastating effects on agriculture, reducing yields which is a loss of income to many families like Tasheni's and has led to food insecurity and malnutrition among young vulnerable children. These droughts have severely affected the economy due to the losses of agriculture and tourism as well as the displacement of many citizens in an attempt for them to seek better living conditions.

Tasheni and her family were forced to migrate to Lusaka, the capital of Zambia as there were better living conditions. Although the Zambian government has attempted to implement measures to address climate change and droughts, it is still not enough. Multiple citizens in the country have been affected by these droughts, which leaves them with no financial security and poor families are unable to make ends meet, no matter how hard they try. Tasheni explained to her friends that the above factors are the reason behind climate change and if we as humans could intensify our efforts to combat climate change, we could potentially reduce the frequency and severity of droughts in Zambia.

In October 2023, Tasheni and her family experienced yet another drought which affected most of the southern half of the country as they received less than the average amount of rainfall, destroying half of the country's maize cultivation. This broke Tasheni as she wanted to see her country develop but this was a large setback. This extremely dry season continued into the new year and by February 2024, the president of Zambia declared a state of emergency due to the severity of this drought and appealed for global assistance. One million households were affected and due to critical food shortages, were unable to meet food needs. Zambia is highly reliant on hydro-electric power and the climate crisis threatens food security, water and energy supply. Tasheni and her family struggled with economic hardships during this dry season but they came to realize that this was a test of endurance and community solidarity.

Lake Kariba, the place where Tasheni came into existence, was suffering profusely. The lake supplies hydro electric energy to Zambia and Zimbabwe but due to the lack of rainfall, drastic power cuts had to be made to both countries which reduced their generating capacity because of the low lake levels. Tasheni's beloved country which already struggled with food shortages now struggled with low power generation caused by the same underlying cause, climate change.

Tasheni realized that the use of hydroelectric power is unsustainable in Zambia as there is not enough water to meet people's daily needs, let alone supply electrical energy to the entire country. This left Tasheni, deep in thought on how to overcome this complication.

For the future of her country, it is up to us to understand the importance of creating a sustainable future. We need a vision of a world where society meets its needs without compromising the ability for future generations to meet their own needs. We need to have our minds at ease that there will be enough water to meet everyone's needs today, tomorrow and in five years from now, but due to Zambia's history with droughts and lack of access to water in rural areas across the country, this makes it rather difficult to achieve.

Tasheni decided to research alternative ways of receiving electricity instead of hydroelectric energy from the Kariba Lake, for if there is not enough water to run the turbines, there will be no electric supply, causing them to shut down. People in Lusaka experience over twelve-hour days without any electricity. Not everyone can afford generators as it is an expensive luxury so
people resort to using candles which has caused many accidents and has taken many lives. Hospitals are not equipped to function without water and electricity, and patients have to wait over four ti six hours to receive medical assistance which has had a critical effect. People have attempted to earn an income by cutting down trees to sell charcoal which has increased deforestation rates and contributes to household air pollution. This vicious cycle affecting Zambia is a consequence of climate change and it is affecting the citizens who have harmed the earth and have contributed to climate change.

The small amount of water the country has, can instead be used on people's daily needs and agriculture for farmers. The severity of the 2023/2024 drought alarmed Tasheni to take action and try to help her country to the best of her ability. At only fifteen years old, Tasheni was able to partake in helping Zambia find an alternative energy source that is sustainable, solar energy. The use of solar energy in Zambia can be highly successful and put a complete end to hydroelectric energy because Zambia receives an abundant amount of sunlight yearly with long photoperiods and the country's geological location presents a rich solar resource that can be used to generate electricity. This can enhance energy security and resilience against climate change impacts.

Another benefit of solar energy is that remote and off- grid areas would be able to benefit from clean and sustainable energy. Tasheni was delighted to find out that by transitioning to solar energy, Zambia could significantly reduce its carbon footprint, mitigate the effects of greenhouse gas, and conserve the county's natural resources. The number of individuals experiencing economic hardship would also decrease as solar projects create new job opportunities and foster innovation in the renewable energy sector. Zambia could really benefit from solar energy by utilizing off-grid solutions for persistent power and can reduce reliance on imported fuels.

Tasheni was able to help her township and multiple others transfer to the use of solar energy. Clinics and hospitals enhanced healthcare delivery and emergency response, schools in the local areas benefited from solar energy solutions and more kids were able to distance learn and excel academically. More importantly, the business sector in Zambia was able to utilize solar energy for manufacturing and producing goods, which has a direct, positive impact on the economy. By harnessing solar energy across Zambia, the country was able to promote energy security, environmental conservation, economic development and social equity. Solar energy is incredibly versatile and it is a valuable asset in advancing the future of Zambia.

Tasheni was able to put an end to the intense dry spells experienced in her country or to stop climate change and global warming, she was able to educate herself and others on the impacts of our actions that have led to Zambia suffering and aid in finding sustainable solutions to the water crisis. Tasheni lives up to her name, of being thankful to God for creating her beautiful country and hopes to inspire people from across the world, to care about the environment, every effort you make towards benefiting the earth, counts.

We as humans have to work together to ensure the resources we have been given never run out. Tasheni has big dreams for Zambia, she hopes to see her country never struggling in a drought again or not having water and electricity, she hopes that more people will think before they harm the earth, and that more people will want to take action in preventing climate change.
You are never too young or too old to be a climate champion, everyone has the power to make a difference. Solar energy promises a sustainable future and development of Zambia as every citizen's needs will be met whilst still being in abundance for future generations to come. Tasheni has high hopes everyone can take inspiration from a young girl like her, who did not have the best upbringing, but continues to persevere through any challenge she stumbles upon, whilst still trying to have a remarkable im-

pact on the environment. She envisions a world where sustainable development has eradicated global warming and droughts in Zambia and other countries, allowing the planet to thrive in a pristine environment.

About the
Voices of Future Generations
Children's Initiative

The Voices of Future Generations Children's Initiative (VoFG CI) is a movement on children's rights and sustainable development. VoFG CI is a unique programme of action that empowers children to promote the UN Convention on the Rights of the Child (CRC) and the World's Sustainable Development Goal agenda (SDGs).

Its mission is to assist children to advance the right to education and literacy globally through the children's book series. Books are authored by children aged eight to twelve, for children aged six and above. These stories from around the world are illustrated and published, and the books disseminated globally to schools and libraries for all children to benefit from the knowledge and insight.

Through its Intergenerational Dialogue Programme, Online Roundtables and Eco-seminars VoFG CI enables children to engage in effective and inspiring communication with experts and global leaders, who are making a positive impact in the fields of children's rights and sustainable development.

For more information, see: vofg.org

Voices of Future Generations Children's Initiative

About the Global Youth Council on Science, Law, and Sustainability

The Global Youth Council on Science, Law and Sustainability was created during COVID-19 lockdown by concerned youth who wanted to continue learning and exploring issues concerning the future science and law needed to tackle the world's most serious sustainability challenges, while their education had been put on pause. These youth came together to establish a council composed of young leaders from many countries, in order to join forces in promoting awareness and education about the SDGs, and fostering youth voices in shaping future science, law and policy that help find sustainable solutions worldwide on all levels. The mission of the Global Youth Council on Science, Law, and Sustainability is to advance the engagement of young people for the public benefit, through inspiration, insights and educational activities, programs and resources on science and law relating to sustainability, innovation and the natural world.

The Global Youth Council on Science, Law and Sustainability has two main objectives:
* to advance the voices and views of young people by developing youth skills, capacities and capabilities, and
* to enable youth to participate in global debates and society as responsible and engaged voices for future generations.

Key programmes of the Global Youth Council include:
* editing Harmony, an online youth journal featuring articles and artwork on the world's Sustainable Development Goals (SDGs),
* editing *Futures*, this biennial anthology of stories by young writers on the SDGs and pathways to more sustainable futures,
* leading projects related to the SDGs in our communities and globally, including through research, consultations, skill and knowledge sharing and action, and
* hosting online and in-person workshops, roundtables and exchanges, social media outreach and awareness raising, meetings with decision makers, and delegations to international negotiations and forums.

For more information, see: harmonyyouthvoices.com

Our International Panel of Judges

Our immense gratitude is owed to the International Judges of the 2024 Global 'Stories for Futures' Competition for Youth Writers which led to this inaugural volume, for their goodwill, careful review and inspiring engagement with the hundreds of stories submitted:

- **Professor Pamela Towela Sambo**, is the Head of Department, Private Law at the University of Zambia, and Chair of the UN Human Rights Commission of Zambia.
- **Professor Freya Baetens** is a Professor of Public International Law at the Faculty of Law, and Director of the International Human Rights Summer School at the Bonavero Institute of Human Rights, also affiliated with the PluriCourts Centre of Excellence (Faculty of Law, Oslo University) and the Europa Institute (Faculty of Law, Leiden University).
- **Professor Marie-Claire Cordonier Segger** is a world-leading scholar and jurist in the field of sustainable development law governance. She is the Senior Director of the Centre for International Sustainable Development Law (CISDL) and serves as Chair in Sustainable Development Law and Policy at the University of Cambridge.
- **Mr. Alistair Henfrey** is the Head of the English Department at Winchester College in the United Kingdom.
- **Dr. Odette Lara-Morales** is the Programme Manager of VoFG CI, an Associate Fellow at CISDL, a Lecturer at the University of Waterloo and a Project Officer with UNA-Canada.
- **Max Lee** is an avid writer, poet, and creative who aspires to help young children find their niches as he did through his love for language and literature. In 2020, in the midst of an epidemic, Max founded a Hong Kong-based youth education company driven by his true joy in educating, Crown Education, teaching with a small group of young visionaries from drama to debate to poetry.
- **Ela Martínez** is an educator with over six years of experience working with teachers, students, and families within and outside of the school context. Ela is the Programme Coordinator of VoFG CI and an Associate Fellow at CISDL.
- **Professor Julie Smith**, Baroness of Newnham is a current member of the House of Lords and an academic specialising in European politics at the University of Cambridge.